Watercolored Pearls by Stacy Hawkins Adams is everything a good story should be: true-to-life and down-to-earth, with God smack-dab in the middle of it all. Stacy's characters and intertwined personal dramas draw readers in from the first page and keep them on the edge of their seats.

—**Kathi Macias**, bestselling author/speaker

This book has everything I love: real people of faith trying to cope with problems and doubts . . . and by the end, a faith made tangible and accessible to everyone. . . . I started reading this in the morning and I couldn't put it down until I finished it . . . you'll do the same thing.

—**Sharon Baldacci**, author of *A Sundog Moment*

Speak to My Heart foretold Stacy Hawkins Adams's potential and gift-edness as a writer and storyteller with longevity. *Watercolored Pearls* is the confirmation. And it is such a beautiful confirmation.

—**Robin Caldwell**, GospelCity.com

In a simple, well-written story, we learn about three different women and their individual stresses, failures, and spiritual tri-umphs. I admired the honesty of Adams's writing. The issues the women face may not be those of every woman, but she makes it clear that the solutions come from the same source.

—**Cecil Murphey**, coauthor of *90 Minutes in Heaven* and more than 100 other books

Through *Watercolored Pearls*, Stacy Hawkins Adams tells a capti-vating story that takes readers through the life journeys of . . . three different women facing three separate issues, trying to find who they are in Christ. During the process, they learn, through the irritants that creep into their lives, that they will struggle, endure, and triumph, becoming greater and stronger women of God than they ever thought they could be. Through their physical, spiritual, and emotional excursions, they find love and comfort in each other as well as in the arms of Christ.

—**Kendra Norman-Bellamy**, founder and president of
KNB Publications, LLC; #1 *Essence* bestselling author

Stacy Hawkins Adams has *set it off* once again. We get more of our girlfriends Serena, Erika, and Tawana, fiercer, finer, and yet more frail than ever. Every young woman needs to hear the message of the *Watercolored Pearls* deftly woven in this novel. Buy this precious gem of a book and a spare to share. It's good like *that*.

—**Claudia Mair Burney**, author of *The Amanda Bell Brown
Mysteries* and *Zora and Nicky: A Novel in Black and White*

Watercolored Pearls is a delightful . . . read. Stacy's story, driven by three loyal girlfriends, reminds us of where true peace and beauty lie. Grab a glass of cold lemonade, curl up under a shady tree, and enjoy!

—**Sharon Ewell Foster**, Christy Award–winning author of
Passing by Samaria and *Abraham's Well*

watercolored pearls

a novel

Stacy Hawkins Adams

Revell
Grand Rapids, Michigan

© 2007 by Stacy Hawkins Adams

Published by Fleming H. Revell
a division of Baker Publishing Group
P.O. Box 6287, Grand Rapids, MI 49516-6287
www.revellbooks.com

Printed in the United States of America

Library of Congress Cataloging-in-Publication Data
Adams, Stacy Hawkins, 1971–
    Watercolored pearls : a novel / Stacy Hawkins Adams.
        p.   cm.
    ISBN 10: 0-8007-3168-9 (pbk.)
    ISBN 978-0-8007-3168-7 (pbk.)
    1. African Americans—Fiction. 2. Faith—Fiction. I. Title.
PS3601.D396W37 2007
813′.6—dc22   2007020550

To three special pearls,
My sisters Barbara Grayson, Sandra Williams,
and Patsy Scott
&
To my brother Waymon,
with love

Again, the Kingdom of Heaven is like a pearl merchant on the lookout for choice pearls. When he discovered a pearl of great value, he sold everything he owned and bought it!

Matthew 13:45–46

1

The scream lodged in Serena McDaniels's throat and refused to budge. She turned left, then right, then stopped to scoop up her son.

One accounted for. In seconds, the other had disappeared.

If fear would release its grip on her vocal chords and allow her to yell, she was sure someone an aisle or two away could help her locate Jaden.

But the words wouldn't come. Serena clutched Jacob to her chest and took off running.

"Ow, Mommy. Too tight!"

Hearing Jacob's voice unleashed hers.

"Jaden?! Jaden? Where are you?"

Serena stood in the middle of Ukrop's, near the grocery store's salad bar, hoping her son would come out of an easy-to-miss hiding spot big enough for a toddler.

She held Jacob closer and squatted to scan the floor beneath the registers.

Jacob tried to wiggle from her grip. Was her heart going to pound through her shirt?

Someone touched her shoulder. She rose and read the tag worn by the man who stood before her. Greg Hill, store manager.

"It's okay, ma'am," he said. "We'll find your son . . . Jaden did I hear you say? He's here somewhere."

Serena nodded, afraid that if she spoke, the waterfall she was struggling to contain would erupt and blur her vision, limiting her ability to find her baby.

Seconds later, she heard a male voice nearby.

"Hey, buddy. I think Mommy's looking for you."

Serena spurted in that direction, with Jacob clinging to her shirt. She peered down every aisle until she saw her curly-haired blessing.

Jaden stood on a nearly empty bottom shelf, stretching his pudgy arm toward a cereal box just out of his reach.

Serena thought she would collapse, but her relief suddenly gave way to frustration.

"Jaden Michael McDaniels, get over here now!"

Instead of climbing down, he turned his big brown eyes on her and smiled. "Life, Mommy. I want Life!"

The man who had discovered the boy lowered Jaden to the floor and patted his head. He took Jaden's hand and led him to Serena.

Jacob wiggled from her arms and slid down her leg to hug his brother. "Jaden found!"

Serena raised her eyes to the stranger. "Thank you, sir. I turned away for a second to grab a can off the shelf, and just that quickly, he climbed out of the cart. Thank you."

The man smiled. "It's okay. He's a boy, and if I'm guessing right, he and his brother here are about two years old. He's doing exactly what he should be doing at this age. I have ten grandchildren and I've been there. Don't worry. You're a good mother."

Serena smiled weakly. Was she really? She thought about the years she had cried and pleaded with God to allow her to bear children. Now that her prayers had been answered, she felt like a frazzled rag doll in need of a Parenting 101 class, instead of the supermom she always dreamed she would be.

The man waved goodbye to the boys and resumed his shopping.

I must have been out of my mind, coming to the grocery store with these boys, and near nap time at that, Serena thought.

She took Jacob and Jaden by the hands and found her shopping cart five rows away. She moved it from the center of the aisle where she had abandoned it, and parked it alongside a shelf.

A store employee approached. "Need some help?"

Serena shook her head. The boys were trying to squirm out of her grip. At this moment, she finally understood why some parents used leashes, a practice she had always criticized.

She knew the young lady would have helped her shop or find an open register to check out, but all she wanted right now was to go home, lie down, and calm her thirty-something nerves.

"I've got to get my sons settled, so I'm not going to buy these items today. I don't have anything perishable in there; can I leave my cart here?"

The clerk smiled. "I don't mind putting everything away for you. Glad you found your son. Kids wander away in here all the time; I guess they're curious."

By the time Serena made it to the minivan and got the two miniature versions of her husband buckled into their car seats, she was sweating. It was a pleasant May morning, but she felt like she was having early onset hot flashes.

Serena buckled her seat belt and closed her eyes. Temporarily losing Jaden in a grocery store wasn't that big of a deal, but then again, it could have been.

Give me some patience, Lord. And some idea of how to manage these rambunctious little boys.

She sighed and waited. Didn't God have a ready answer for her?

Her cell phone chimed and she laughed out loud.

"Alright now, Daddy," she said, using the name she often called God. "That was fast."

Serena looked at the number and saw that it was Micah. "Hi there."

"Hey, love. Where are you? Did you forget that Bethany was stopping by the house today to pick up that package for Ian? She tracked me down here at the church and said you weren't home."

The boys grew louder in the backseat. They giggled and practiced moves with the miniature action figures she kept in a small basket for them. Right now, the plastic toys were scattered everywhere.

"Serena, you there?"

"One of your sons did a disappearing act in Ukrop's just now," she said. "I found him trying to grab his favorite cereal on a shelf he couldn't reach."

Micah's rumbling laughter irritated her.

"I'm glad you find it so funny," she said. "I thought I was going to have a heart attack. And, I have some bad

12

news: I left the basket in the store, filled with the ingredients I needed for tonight's dinner and for the lunch I was planning to serve Miss Bethany. It's only 10:30 anyway. She's early."

She knew Micah was waiting until she finished her tirade.

"I'll call Bethany and tell her she can get the package some other time," he said. "Sounds like you and the boys need a nap."

Serena opened her eyes and breathed deeply. Whenever she felt herself careening over the edge, Micah always helped her pull herself together.

"I've got men's Bible study tonight, but I'll get home as soon as I can."

"I know you mean well, babe," Serena said, more calmly this time, "but your 'early' still means after dinner, and after bath time."

She didn't intend to make him feel guilty, but he didn't understand how exhausting it was to spend 24/7 with two kids so full of life that by the time they'd been awake for two hours, she was ready to hide in a closet and regroup. He also didn't know how bad she felt for having those thoughts.

"You're right," he said. "My early is still late. Don't worry about preparing dinner. Give the boys something light and eat what you want—the leftover roast from yesterday. I'll eat whatever I can find when I get there. I'm gonna run and call Bethany back about Ian's package. Love ya."

"Love you too, babe," Serena said. "Sorry I'm so cranky."

"Don't sweat it. Gotta run."

Serena clicked off the cell phone and turned to look at her sons. Their identical eyebrows, noses, smiles, and dark chocolate complexions stole her heart every time she glimpsed them.

A few years ago, she had clutched her flat belly in grief, wailing for God to fill it with a child. He had given her a double blessing, and she was grateful. She was also torn, though, because loving them seemed to be draining the life out of her.

2

Erika Tyler Wilson stared at the unopened greeting card and debated her options. If she tore it up now, Aaron would be watching and want to know why. If she waited, she might actually be tempted to read the romantic musings scripted by the card manufacturer, as well as the handwritten message she knew Elliott had neatly penned—again.

She shifted in her seat and continued sorting through the mail while she waited for the pasta to cook.

Aaron sat across from her and colored a worksheet his preschool teacher had given him as homework. When she sighed heavily and picked up the card again, he looked up.

"What, Mommy?"

She laughed and tweaked his nose. "Why do you want to know, little man? Are you going to handle this for me?"

"Yes," he said with a straight face. "Tell me so I can fix it."

He had just turned four, but Erika regularly informed anyone who asked his age that he was going on forty. He was what her friend and surrogate mother Charlotte called

15

an "old soul," and Erika agreed—he *was* wise beyond his years.

"Nothing for you to worry about, sweetie," Erika said. "Mommy's just reading the mail. Finish your homework."

She rose from the table and went to the stove to stir the marinara sauce in one pot and the pasta in another. She zoned in on the circular motions and tried not to be angry because of the letter. Every two weeks, she went through the same emotions.

Memories of the fear, the beatings, and the sickness of loving someone who hurt her rushed forth.

She thought about Naomi's Nest, the shelter she had called home for nearly a year. Kodak-like images of that period flashed through her mind: the joy of giving birth to Aaron; the anguish of handing him over six weeks later for Serena and Micah to raise; interning at D. Haven Interior Designs to learn the craft from senior designer Gabrielle Donovan and the company's owner, Derrick Haven. Falling in love with God for the first time. And eventually, with. . . .

Erika laid the wooden spoon on the stovetop and abruptly walked away. She returned to the kitchen table, still lost in her reflections. Aaron was so engrossed in coloring images that began with the letter *Y* that he didn't notice.

"Look, Mommy! All done now and ready to eat!"

He gripped the paper, stood up on his chair, and leaned toward Erika to hand it over.

"Good job, Aaron," she said and smiled. "Dinner will be ready in a few minutes."

She grabbed him around the waist and lifted him across

the table, into her arms. Erika hugged him tightly and planted a loud kiss on his soft cheek.

She sat back in the chair and smiled down at her son. Despite the darkness of her days as Elliott Wilson's wife, God had created something magnificent from the best of the both of them. Aaron had been graced with their similar honey complexions and thin frames; he was the perfect combination of his parents.

When he spent time with Elliott during supervised visits, no one doubted that the two were father and son. Yet put the boy next to Erika and there was the same effect—he looked just like his mom.

He was still young enough that the life that had been crafted for him was the only normal he knew. It made sense to Aaron that the bedroom he slept in every night used to be Aunt Serena's when she was a girl, growing up in this North Richmond ranch-style house.

"Doesn't everybody have someone like Aunt Serena and Uncle Micah?" he once asked Erika, when a friend at pre-school moved into a new house her parents had built.

Erika snuggled with her son until he squirmed away.

"What's in here, Mommy? A birthday card?"

He had noticed the pink envelope that bore Elliott's Chesterfield County return address. Thank goodness he couldn't read.

Before she could dream up an appropriate answer, the doorbell saved her. Erika walked to the living room and stood on her tiptoes to peer through the front door's peep-hole.

Gabrielle was just in time for dinner. She opened the

door and headed back toward the kitchen. "Had to work later than usual?"

"Yeah," Gabrielle replied. "Had an evening meeting to finalize the papers for the Mitchell deal. The spaghetti smells good."

Gabrielle lived two hours away, in Northern Virginia, where the main office of D. Haven Designs was located. When the interior design firm that also employed Erika opened a Richmond office two years ago, Gabrielle began traveling to the capital city twice a week.

Erika worked full-time in Richmond and insisted that Gabrielle stay in the extra bedroom of the house she was renting from Serena and Micah.

The arrangement worked well, for a number of reasons. Among them was that it meant she didn't always have to do "Elliott watch" alone.

Gabrielle took her briefcase to the guest room and returned seconds later. She strolled to the kitchen sink and washed her hands with the antibacterial soap perched on the window ledge. When Aaron leapt from the table to find the tennis ball a neighbor had given him earlier that day, the stack of mail caught Gabrielle's eye.

"Another card, huh? Wonder what he's saying this time," she said softly, mindful that Aaron would return in a few seconds.

Erika shrugged and set three plates on the table, including a miniature one bearing Scooby-Doo's image.

"He keeps saying he's a different man," she said. "I see him at church, serving as an usher. I know he provides free legal counsel on small cases for members who can't afford representation.

"But I don't trust him. He says he's giving me space, but these cards keep coming," Erika said. "Like clockwork. On the first and fifteenth of every month. The day of the month we met and the day of the month we married."

Gabrielle shook her head and scanned the hallway for Aaron. "I hope you're keeping them. For evidence."

"Most of them, unless I get frustrated and rip them apart," Erika laughed sheepishly. "That's happened a few times." She picked up the envelope and fingered it.

"Why not read it? I know I've heard it all before."

She tore open the card and sighed at the cover: "'If love had another name, it would be yours . . .'" Her eyes widened when she read the message inside.

"What?" Gabrielle asked.

"He says he's found someone else. He wants a divorce."

3

Tawana Carter hated begging. Tonight, though, she couldn't help it. She stood at the door outside of her apartment, trying not to stare at the muscles rippling through her date's crisp white oxford shirt and denim jeans, and silently pleaded with God to give her the strength to say no.

"You tired?" Grant Parker peered at her over the top of his wire-rimmed glasses and let a slow smile travel across his broad, handsome face. His deep brown eyes locked with hers.

In the thirty seconds she hesitated before responding, Tawana thought about Misha, possibly still awake inside, and how her daughter didn't need to accidentally meet another one of Mommy's "friends." She knew her mother would have her door ajar, listening for a stranger to tiptoe down the hallway. She recalled how she usually felt the day after.

Thank you, God.

Tawana shrugged and returned Grant's full smile. His grin noticeably faded when she replied.

"You know, I am a little tired. It's been a long week. Thanks for a wonderful evening, though. It was fascinating to learn more about the goals of a future plastic surgeon—in and out of the operating room."

Grant leaned toward Tawana and lightly hugged her. She accepted, but she really wanted a kiss.

"You're pretty interesting yourself, soon-to-be Attorney Carter. I'll call you."

Tawana offered another smile and hoped he hadn't noticed her gripping the doorknob behind her. She watched him swagger toward the elevator and returned his wave before he stepped aboard and disappeared.

"I need a drink," she mumbled and inserted her key into the lock. Seconds later, she stood before her pantry, debating which of the two bottles of wine appealed to her tonight. She needed just enough to ease the familiar loneliness and inadequacy that routinely engulfed her, until sleep delivered some peace.

She reached for the merlot, a Christmas gift a professor had "regifted" to her for helping organize his student files.

When a set of golden-hued arms encircled her waist, she turned toward Misha and gave her daughter a hug.

"Hi, baby. What are you still doing up?"

It was Friday, but her mother sometimes made Misha go to bed on time during the weekend too.

"Gram and I just finished playing Monopoly. I'm bored. Can we play checkers?"

Tawana smiled at the slender, sandy-haired seven-year-old version of herself. Their matching fair skin, sprinkle of freckles across the bridge of the nose, light brown eyes, and long legs often made people do double takes. The only thing that prevented mother and daughter from being mistaken for sisters was Tawana's curvier hips and advantage in height. Their sixteen-year age difference seemed slighter when the youthful Tawana didn't wear makeup.

She rested her glass and wine bottle on the counter near the sink while she searched through a cluttered drawer for a corkscrew.

"You're always bored. It's nine thirty and past your bedtime. Go."

Misha ignored the instruction and sauntered over to Tawana, where she watched her mother open the merlot.

"Gram's probably in bed by now. When she heard you coming through the door, she said she was going to call it a night. I'm not sleepy. Tell me about your date."

Tawana paused with her wine glass halfway to her lips and looked at her daughter. "How did you know I had a date?"

"Gram told me. She said she was going to stay up until you made it home, to make sure you behaved."

Tawana gulped her wine and turned away from her daughter. She bit her bottom lip. "Misha, we'll talk about it later. Go to your room. Read a book or something until you fall asleep."

"But Ma, I—"

Tawana gave her the "You heard what I said" glare. Misha rolled her eyes and stormed out of the kitchen.

"Spend the rest of the night with yourself, then!"

"Little girl, don't make me come after you!"

Tawana slammed her glass on the Formica countertop, spilling some of its contents. She strode toward Misha's bedroom but stopped halfway down the narrow hall when the door ricocheted against its frame.

"I know that little second grader didn't," Tawana muttered and put her hands on her hips. She was heading toward Misha's room when her mother breezed past her.

"I'm glad you didn't stay out all night this time. That girl is watching you." Ms. Carter disappeared into her dark room and gently closed the door.

Tawana crossed the hall, raised her fist to pound on her mother's door, then stopped. She didn't have the energy to fight tonight. Mama always had something negative to say, no matter what she did.

And sooner or later, she was going to have to deal with Misha's rebellion. The girl wasn't a preteen yet, and she already had begun acting out. Who did she think she was, talking like that to an adult, to her mother of all people?

Tawana changed courses and went toward Misha's room instead. She turned the doorknob and peered inside. Misha sat on her bed with her arms and ankles crossed. She was facing the mirror above her dresser and scowling at herself.

"You owe me an apology," Tawana said. She leaned against the door and waited.

Misha lowered her head and mumbled inaudibly.

"Excuse me?"

"I'm sorry, Mommy."

"Put on your pajamas, brush your teeth, and go to sleep."

Tawana left Misha's bedroom door open and returned to the kitchen. She should be using this time more wisely, reviewing briefs or doing research for an upcoming paper. Oh well.

She filled the near-empty wine glass to the rim with more merlot before shutting off the lights and sauntering to her bedroom.

"Good night, Misha. Love you," she called to her daughter.

There was a long pause.

"Love you too, Mommy."

Tawana savored the wine and turned her thoughts to Grant. Her lips curved into a smile as she recounted their dinner and brief evening stroll afterward. She'd have to call Elizabeth tomorrow to thank her for connecting the two of them. Some friends knew how to arrange a blind date.

Tawana set her glass on the nightstand. She slipped off her high-heeled sandals and the sleeveless linen top and low-waisted black capris she had changed into after her torts class. She hadn't known what to expect from her date, but she had wanted to make a memorable first impression, one that lingered.

"Thrilled" inadequately described what she felt when the chiseled, bronze-complexioned Grant had greeted her on the steps of the law school library. They spent the evening at Veronique, not far from Harvard's campus, enjoying the restaurant's harpist and melt-in-your-mouth food.

Now she tossed the clothes near the door, on top of the pile to be laundered. She tucked away her shoes and rifled through the armoire for her red pajama shorts and matching top.

Tawana slid into the jammies and flipped on the bathroom light. Her thoughts kept her company while she completed her nightly facial cleansing routine, brushed her teeth, and wrapped her shoulder-length hair in a scarf.

She tried to recall a time when she hadn't turned to something alcoholic to relax her after a long study session, or just before a nerve-wracking encounter, like tonight's date.

Minutes later, she plopped on top of her bed and polished off the last of her drink. She snuggled under the covers, thankful that her mother hadn't cranked up the air tonight. Usually she'd be shivering. Her head sank deep into the pillow.

Sleep was coming quickly. Until the shrill ring of the telephone jolted her to attention. Tawana groaned and groped the nightstand with her fingers. She grabbed the cordless phone and cleared her throat, in case it was Grant.

"Hello?"

Too late. The caller had already been directed to voice mail.

She waited a few minutes before dialing into the automated system to retrieve her messages. *Should have checked them anyway when I got home,* she thought.

There were three new messages.

A call that morning from her hair salon reminded her of an early appointment the next day. Good. She was overdue for a touch-up.

Elizabeth had called around 6 p.m. "I can't wait to get details, so I'm calling ahead of time to remind you to call me tomorrow! Let me know what you thought of Mr. Hunky. Did I do well? I might not be a sister, but I know how to pick 'em!"

Tawana laughed out loud and erased the message. She'd

have to school her Irish-American friend. It was "sista," not "sister."

The next message woke her up.

"Hello, Ms. Carter, this is Emery Goodwin with Wallace, Jones and Johns Law Firm." Tawana reclined against the headboard as she listened to the rest of the message.

"We're delighted that you've accepted a spot in our summer internship program. Specific instructions and details will be coming shortly, through the mail, but I'm touching base to see what your other needs may be while you're in Richmond this summer, such as transportation and lodging. Please call me on Monday so we can go over logistics for the twelve weeks that you'll be part of our team."

Tawana placed the cordless phone on the charger and fell back onto her pillow, wide awake now. If she were a typical law school student, she'd be beside herself with anticipation over this internship at one of the nation's top law firms.

She wasn't the average twenty-three-year-old, though. She had a child. She shared a cramped apartment with her mother, who was struggling to be supportive in an intellectually and culturally foreign world. And she dealt with classmates who she was sure considered her a charity case, able to skate by because of her stereotypical circumstances.

On most days Tawana was thrilled and proud to have landed such a prestigious summer gig. Most of her classmates viewed this type of opportunity as part of the Harvard package, but she hadn't taken her selection for granted.

On other days, she wrestled with where she hoped this path was leading and where she now found herself. The inconsistencies always seemed more apparent in this drab and drafty Somerville apartment just outside of Boston.

Ms. Goodwin's call reminded Tawana that accepting the internship had been "phase one." To succeed, she needed to follow through on the next step—finding a place to stay, for herself and for Misha. Mama wouldn't mind moving in with one of her siblings in Richmond for the summer, but Tawana had no intention of exposing Misha to her relatives, who still lived in dire circumstances in the city's northside projects.

Instead, she was banking on Serena's and Micah's big hearts. Now she had to find the courage to ask them.

4

Serena stood in the foyer of her Ginter Park home in North Richmond and surveyed her surroundings. Her eyes moved from the eclectic mix of art that graced the walls to the oversized crystal vase of fresh flowers resting on the pedestal table in the center of the floor. Everything sparkled and was in its proper place.

She hadn't fared so well last week, when Bethany stopped by unexpectedly and invited herself in for a visit. Miss Diva didn't mask her dismay at the jumble of toys, newspapers, and mail splayed across the kitchen.

"You should invest in a maid, Serena. My goodness."

She spoke sweetly to Jacob and Jaden but recoiled when one of the twins tried to touch her with pudding-sticky fingers.

"I'm wearing Prada today, little one," she said and backed away. She smiled at Serena apologetically. "It's dry-clean only."

This time, Serena would be prepared for the white glove test. That is, if she could keep the boys from wrecking the place over the next twenty-four hours.

"Why am I so concerned about what she thinks, anyway?" she said aloud and sprayed a vertical mirror with glass cleaner for the fourth time.

Tawana's tinkling laughter startled her. Serena turned and glared at her young friend, who stood in the dining room entrance, adjacent to the foyer, holding a soiled cloth in her hand.

"I've been wondering that, too," Tawana said. "You—no, we—have been cleaning around here like the governor is coming, since I arrived this morning. You're hosting a Sunday afternoon cookout tomorrow, not a formal dinner."

"What are you trying to tell me? To chill out?" Serena laughed and resumed polishing surfaces that already sparkled. "You haven't met Bethany."

Tawana ticked off the chores she had completed on her fingers. "The bathroom is spotless. The dining room table and buffet have been polished. I've swept the kitchen—again. And most of the boys' toys are tucked away."

She walked over to Serena and tugged the dusting cloth from Serena's hand.

"I've figured it out now," Tawana said, feigning disappointment. "You wanted me to come down for the weekend to work. I feel like I'm in high school again, completing my after-school chores. We should have put Misha to work."

Serena gave her a light hug. She still found it hard to believe that the young lady she had mentored through the highs and lows of high school was studying at Harvard. Tawana had grown up so much, and yet in many ways, she still seemed so vulnerable.

"What are you talking about, T? It's a tradition for you and Misha to spend Micah's birthday weekend with us.

"Misha's up there with those two-year-old boys—believe me, she *is* working. Thanks for all of your help. I can't get anything done around here anymore with the two of them underfoot."

Tawana nodded. "I remember how hard it was to concentrate on homework and take care of Misha at the same time. I thought I would go crazy. But it got better as she got older."

Serena dumped her cleaning supplies in a cloth-lined wicker basket and cradled it in her arms. She motioned for Tawana to follow her through the kitchen into the garage.

"I hope so," she said. "But it's hard to see beyond each day's frantic pace. I fall into bed exhausted every night."

Serena nudged Tawana with her elbow. "I can't believe I'm taking parenting advice from my little T. The tables have turned!"

She tucked the cleaning supplies on an eye-level shelf and led the way back to the kitchen, where she headed toward the refrigerator. "Let me pull together something for lunch."

Serena paused and cocked her head to the side, with her hand resting on the refrigerator door handle.

"When it's quiet like this, I get worried," Serena said. "Either they're up there sleeping or doing something they probably shouldn't be."

Tawana laughed. "Those two could probably convince Misha to do anything. They were watching *Dora the Ex-*

plorer when I came down a few minutes ago. I'll run up and check on them."

As Tawana climbed the stairs two by two, Serena called after her, "Want a BLT or chicken salad sandwich?"

"The first choice," Tawana said.

"Me too."

"And three and four."

Serena turned toward the kitchen's side entrance and shook her head at Micah and Ian standing in the doorway. She glanced at the digital clock on the microwave. "I didn't hear you guys come in. Been gone four hours, but sure enough, you come back just in time to eat. Did you even hear what the first choice was?"

Micah walked over to Serena and kissed her lips.

Ian laughed. "Nope, and we don't care. Whatever you cook, we'll like."

He plopped into a chair at the small table in the breakfast nook. Serena opened the fridge to grab the bacon, and Micah reached around her for two bottles of water.

"Tiger Woods didn't have nothing on me today, baby. Neither did Ian."

He set one of the bottles of water in front of Ian and slapped his friend on the back.

Ian was preparing his comeback when Tawana descended the stairs and waved at the men.

"The boys are sprawled out on the playroom floor, sleeping like it's midnight," she said. "Looks like Misha convinced them to play school, and as the teacher, she enforced a naptime that she wanted to sample."

The four adults laughed.

"Misha needs to visit more often," Micah said.

"Amen to that," Serena said lightheartedly. "If that's what I need to do to get them to settle down, maybe *I'll* start playing the teacher."

She hoped her smile hid her frustration. On most days, the naps they eventually took came after a tantrum or two, or after Serena became so desperate that she'd promise them after-dinner ice cream or some other treat—a practice she had scolded young mothers for using when she had been executive director of the Children's Art Coalition.

A seven-year-old does a better job than I can of getting them to cooperate.

She shifted her attention to Micah to stave off the rising resentment. "So you beat your best buddy here, huh?"

Ian shook his head dismissively. "Don't believe that man. He's a lying preacher if I ever saw one."

Tawana took the mayonnaise, lettuce, and tomato Serena juggled in her arms.

"I'm staying out of this one," she said.

Serena spread the bacon across a plate, covered it with a paper towel, and slid it into the microwave. She pulled out a colander to wash the lettuce.

"Have you two been talking smack all morning?" Before they could answer, she switched gears. "While you debate that answer, can you make sure we have everything straight for tomorrow? Enough tables and chairs, sodas, propane? I'll call you when lunch is ready."

Micah and Ian took their bottles of water and headed outside.

"Come on, man. You can help me write my sermon too," Micah told Ian and laughed.

As their voices trailed off in a conversation still focused

on golf, Tawana joined Serena at the sink and picked up a knife to cut the lettuce.

"You'll find this funny," Serena said softly to Tawana. "Ian can come in here with the house looking like a jungle and I don't flinch. But all that cleaning we did earlier? It's for his pretty wife."

Tawana laughed. "Serena, I'm beginning to worry about you," she said. "Am I going to have to stop leaning on you to steer me right? Becoming a mother has worn you down."

If only she knew, Serena thought.

"Keep me in prayer, girl. This full-fledged grown-up needs it every day—even a preacher's wife," Serena said, and then turned the conversation back to Tawana. "When are you picking up your mother?"

"Miss Brenda said she'd bring her back," Tawana said. "They were so happy to see each other that they'll probably be talking late into the night. Don't be offended if Mama misses church and your party tomorrow. I overheard her agreeing to spend Sunday with one of my aunts."

"No problem," Serena said. "Are you going by to see them before you leave?"

Tawana shrugged. "They haven't changed much; still struggling to make ends meet, still living on the edge."

Serena raised an eyebrow. "Don't take the people who love you for granted, T," she said. "Been there, done that."

Serena thought about all the years she had wasted being angry with her mother because her father was someone other than she'd been led to believe. By the time she let go of the bitterness, she and Mama had little time left. They had forgiven each other before Mama died, but Serena's regret lingered to this day.

It still brought tears to her eyes. She changed the subject again. "How's Ms. Carter adjusting to Boston? I know last winter was hard on her."

"It's difficult for her to be so far away from everyone and everything she knows," Tawana said. "Charlottesville was one thing. When I was at U.Va., she could catch a bus to Richmond on the weekends to visit her friends or church. In Boston she doesn't care for the people whose houses she cleans. And she hasn't made any friends, probably because she thinks the people there are standoffish. The real problem is, she won't take the time to find out differently."

Serena looked up from the deep fryer she had plugged in to cook some fries. "This is why my hips are holding on to that baby fat, even though the 'babies' are almost two and a half," she told Tawana. "And Misha?"

"Misha is getting hard to handle," Tawana said and sighed. "She gets mad because I'm gone a lot, but when I'm not in class, I'm studying."

Her cell phone vibrated in its holster on her waist. She clapped her hands when she saw the number.

"It's Grant!" she told Serena. "Should I answer?"

Serena poured frozen potato wedges into the bubbling oil without responding.

"What?" Tawana asked. She looked down at her phone. "I missed his call! I hope he's leaving a message."

Serena paused and faced Tawana. "You know I'm proud of you and all that you're accomplishing. It isn't easy. But maybe you need to slow down. Misha still needs you, too."

The fiery response flaring in Tawana's eyes surprised Serena.

"Mama's there for her when I can't be," Tawana said. "I don't know how else I'm going to make the grade if I don't put in the hours and pull my weight with my study groups. This is the way it's always been done. It's none of the other students' fault that I'm a mother."

Serena's heart softened. So that's what this was about. She'd been there herself at about the same age, when she'd learned the truth about her father. Instead of it being the man in the cemetery whose name was on her birth certificate, her real father, Melvin Gates, attended her childhood church with his wife, Althea, and served as a deacon.

Tawana's situation wasn't the same, but the shame and self-doubt were. She hoped her friend wasn't foolish enough to run from God, like she'd been determined to do.

Talk to her.

Serena knew what that whisper meant.

She motioned for Tawana to join her at the table.

"You were a teenage mother, T. It is what it is. Misha is a beautiful girl, you've earned a full ride to Harvard Law School—you have everything going for you. Don't get hung up on things you can't change. The admissions board knew who they were getting when they admitted you. They chose you because of who you are."

Tawana hinted at a smile. "I know, Serena. But I can't help my schedule. This is law school. Plus I'm getting a master's in public policy too. It's a grueling pace."

"Misha's only seven," Serena said. "You have to spend some special time with her, just the two of you—no Gram and no 'significant other.'"

Ms. Carter had told her about the times Tawana had gone on dates and stayed out overnight. Once, she'd let a man sleep at the apartment. Worse than that, Tawana had introduced several of her friends to Misha, leaving the girl confused when they disappeared.

Lord, please don't let this child wind up with another baby.

"And speaking of time, you know what else I'm going to say is important."

Tawana stared at her.

"As busy and as stressful as your life is right now, I hope you're still praying every morning. Your faith isn't just for Sunday morning shouting, you know."

Tawana smiled politely.

"Let me stop before I start sounding like a Holy Roller," Serena said and rose from her seat. "Just know that I'm preaching to myself too."

Tawana joined Serena at the sink, where Serena washed the few dishes stacked there while waiting on the fries to cook. She grabbed a dish towel and began drying the glasses and silverware as Serena passed them to her. They worked in silence, each lost in her thoughts.

Serena reviewed their afternoon together and felt guilty.

The way I've acted today, what right do I have to tell her anything?

Who was she to be giving advice when her efforts to raise her boys left her feeling like a failure most days? How could she encourage Tawana to stay focused when she let the wife of her husband's best friend get her all worked up?

"You know what, T?" she finally said. "I've been tripping today. I guess I have issues with Bethany coming to my creaky old house with 'lots of potential,' when always talking about her wonderful life in her fabulc interior decorated, suburban West End mansion.

"Plus, I'm stressing about Micah's relatives doing a critique of my household skills. I'm home with the boys full-time, so I should have it all together, shouldn't I?"

She smiled wanly. "I'm still trying to figure out how in an eight-year span I've drifted from a successful advertising executive to a focused nonprofit leader to a not-so-on-top-of-things stay-at-home mom."

"You're doing a great job, Serena. What are you talking about?" Tawana asked. "And what's this about Micah's family coming to visit? Aren't you cool with his parents?"

Serena paused. "His parents, yes. The rest of them, I don't know. Micah's older sister is visiting with her son and daughter for two weeks this summer. That's just what I need—more kids underfoot when I can barely keep my two in check."

An odd look crossed Tawana's face. Serena could have sworn it was fear.

5

Whatever doubts, frustrations, or guilt Serena battled during the week, she always felt better when she brought them to the Lord. Now if she could just learn to leave them with him and keep pushing forward.

"When we talk to God, wherever we are and whenever we need him, he's listening," Micah told the congregation this morning as he prepared to lead them in prayer. "God's not like our family and friends, sometimes available by cell phone or email and sometimes not. He doesn't love us one day and turn his back on us the next. Bring your heart to God. Bring your fears, your worries, and your thanksgiving."

People throughout the crowded gym stood on their feet and linked hands while the choir softly sang, "All I wanna do is bless your name . . ."

Before she closed her eyes, Serena scanned the room and silently thanked God—again—for growing Micah's ministry. God had swelled the congregation from a handful of members who lived in the Stillwell Community to about a thousand, who came from throughout metro Richmond on

Sundays and during the week to fellowship in this troubled neighborhood.

Serena knew numbers didn't matter to Micah; that was one of the reasons he had been fired by a church across the river. Standing Rock Community Church had wanted fame and fortune, and under the leadership of Micah's replacement, Jason Lyons, they appeared to be achieving their goal. You couldn't live in Richmond and miss the billboards touting the church's national presence on the Praises Go Up Gospel Network or the yellow Hummers that Standing Rock officials used to transport members to and from Sunday services.

"You're God's best! At Standing Rock, we treat you that way!"

Serena sometimes teased Micah by pointing a finger at him and reciting that slogan, which was emblazoned on all of the SUVs, except for Pastor Lyons's.

"Believe me," Micah would respond wryly, "I know how they treasure people. Until you've been kicked out with no warning, you haven't been given the royal treatment."

In the three years since Micah had founded New Hope Community Ministries, God had been good. New Hope's membership had grown large enough for him to earn full-time wages, which he supplemented with substitute teaching or seasonal post office work.

The ministry's focus remained on the residents of some of South Richmond's toughest streets, but word spread quickly throughout the region about the blend of worship and local mission work taking place there.

Teenage mothers were paired with older women who supported them in parenting. Adults looking for jobs went through a four-week etiquette and interview-training program, sponsored by two church members who worked for the state employment commission. Micah frequently visited juvenile court with kids from the area and asked the presiding judge to send them through the church's Rites of Passage adolescent mentoring program instead of to detention. He agreed to report youths who didn't show up on time and participate in every session.

Serena arranged for homeless women and children living in some of the shelters in the area to be transported by bus to New Hope's services on Sunday and to Bible study on Wednesdays. Those children were paired with reading buddies, who gave them a new book to keep each week.

Serena's longtime friend Erika had relinquished her real estate license some time ago and was now pursuing her love of interior design, but once a month Erika hosted a first-time home buyers clinic for the church in conjunction with officials from the state's housing development agency.

As quickly as the roster of members grew, so did the ministries.

"If God has blessed you with the gift of financial wisdom, then share it," Micah said one Sunday. "If you're a teacher, find your niche and help with our spiritual education team. If you have a gift for praying, come each week to teach others how to talk to God; then lead them to God's heart."

Those who visited or became members had no doubt where Micah stood on the issues of service and faith. He taught the congregation that when they used their gifts and talents to help others, they were doing more than just earning the right to call themselves "Christians." They were modeling Jesus, who healed the sick, fed five thousand, and gave hope to people who were condemned by others.

At New Hope, they weren't just studying Jesus's love for others; they were seeking ways to share it.

Micah and Serena had been forced to practice what he preached when Erika's estranged husband Elliott began attending services Sunday after Sunday and eventually became an official member.

Elliott joined the usher board and helped seat visitors and distribute bulletins. It was odd to see this corporate lawyer, in his Brooks Brothers suit, guiding visitors and members to rows of folding chairs in the elementary school gym that doubled as New Hope's sanctuary. Pretty-boy handsome, Elliott seemed not to notice his effect on the women who requested church fans or directions to the ladies' room or a good Christian hug just so they could get his attention.

Somehow, every Sunday he managed to work his way over to Erika. Serena was convinced he had volunteered for the position just so he'd be able to scan the congregation and keep an eye on her during the service.

"Want to join me after church for lunch?" he routinely asked, but Erika always declined. Serena sometimes voiced her wish that he would find another church so that Erika could worship in peace. After all, she was the best friend of the First Lady.

Micah had scolded her.

"At least the man is in church and not lurking outside Erika's windows."

But Elliott had been serious about trying to win his wife

back. Since her return to Richmond two years ago to work for D. Haven Interior Designs, he had taken anger management classes and had mailed her a copy of his graduation certificate. He requested regular visits with Aaron and didn't protest when Erika insisted that they be supervised.

"I deserve that," he had said. "As long as I get to see my son. And I want you to know, I haven't given up hope on us being a family someday."

Yet Erika remained skeptical.

"He knows how to manipulate a situation to get what he wants," she warned Micah and Serena. "But I've got my life back now; I'm not running anymore."

Serena wasn't so sure. Erika might not be fleeing from Elliott, but she seemed to be letting her next best chance at happiness slip through her fingers. Derrick wasn't just her boss; he had cared about her for a long time.

Serena was stunned, however, to see him sitting in the congregation today. Erika usually didn't do anything that might inflame Elliott, like inviting another man to church. What gave?

Derrick leaned toward Erika after prayer and whispered in her ear. Serena had a clear view of them from where she sat, in a section of chairs set off to the side for choir members.

Serena was certain Erika didn't realize it, but when she was with Derrick, her demeanor changed. The nervous tension and anxiousness that usually enveloped her fell away. She laughed genuinely. She let her son play with Derrick without worrying about Aaron's safety or well-being.

To any stranger looking at the petite, Halle Berry–

look-alike Erika, the trim and muscular Derrick, and the happy-go-lucky Aaron, they seemed like a sweet little family. Serena knew if Derrick had his way, that would have been the case by now.

There was the matter of Erika's marriage, though, complicated by her newfound faith.

"Everything I read in the Bible about ending marriage refers to God not being pleased with divorce," she repeatedly told Serena and even Derrick, when he had finally professed a more-than-friendly interest in her. "I may want to leave Elliott and move on with my life, but God may want something different. I have to wait on him to lead me."

Here she sat today, though, in church with a man who was ready to be part of her future. And where was Elliott?

Today's sermon had better be good.

Serena glanced at Micah, who sat with his eyes closed in meditation as he prepared to speak after another song from the choir. The father of her children still had the power to make her knees weak. That was something else to thank God for.

When Serena caught Erika looking her way, she balled her fist up and held it to her ear, her silent gesture for "Call me—we have to talk."

Erika lowered her head. Serena knew something big had happened.

6

"So Elliott asks for a divorce and you call Derrick."

Serena didn't mean to sound cynical, but Erika's reaction to the greeting card and note she had received from Elliott last week raised some concerns. Erika lived in a battered women's shelter for a year to get away from this man. Now she was trying to make him jealous?

"This must mean that you still care about him, to do something so impulsive."

Erika glared at Serena. "You're on a roll today, girlfriend. I'm not the twins, remember?"

Serena grabbed more toys to take to the backyard and walked over to her friend.

"Don't try that reverse psychology on me, Erika," she said, eyeing Erika's back as Erika retrieved an Elmo sprinkler from a corner of the garage. "It's just that you've been so cautious these past couple of years, so focused on how you want to move forward and with whom, I don't recall any talk about reuniting with Elliott. You told Derrick you needed your space until you worked everything out.

"Now that Elliott seems to finally be ending his fixation

with you, you're playing high school games. You know if he had been at church today and had seen Derrick sitting next to you, holding his son, he probably would have flipped. Forget anger management training."

Erika led the way out of the garage, toting folding chairs under each arm. They were almost as big as she was, Serena noted. And now that Serena carried an extra thirty pounds on her frame that she couldn't seem to shed, she towered over her best friend like the Jolly Green Giant.

"How many more chairs do we need?" Erika asked between heavy breaths.

"Enough for my crew; yours; Ian, Bethany, and Victoria; and Melvin's family, in case they stop by on the way out of town."

Serena hoped they would. Jacob and Jaden loved their grandpop more than anything. One fast twirl on Melvin's shoulders and a try at guessing how he magically moved a quarter from one hand to the other would be the biggest thrill of their day.

The two women worked side by side, positioning chairs under the folding tables Micah had placed in the shadiest area of the large, fenced backyard. The property wasn't as spacious as what Serena and Micah had owned when they lived in Cobblestone Creek, one of Chesterfield County's well-regarded communities, but Serena was content.

She struggled with motherhood these days, but she hadn't forgotten the pain of the miscarriages and the deep longing for a baby that she'd experienced while she lived in the mini-mansion. She knew what mattered.

The women slowly crossed the yard on their way back to the kitchen. Erika finally filled the silence.

"I don't know, Serena. I'm just torn." She looked toward the patio, where Derrick leaned against the brick wall of the house and talked to Micah, who was basting chicken and ribs.

"Elliott's cards come so often now that I usually just toss them aside," she said. "But Gabrielle was there that evening, and curiosity got the better of us. Part of me thinks he's just calling my bluff, to see what I will do."

Erika turned and looked at Serena. "I mean, has he been sending me cards all this time and secretly dating someone else? Who is she?"

They walked through the garage to enter the kitchen.

"I'll say it again," Serena said, a little less sternly this time. "Seems to me like you care a little too much."

Erika busied herself with removing cans of soda from the refrigerator and sticking them in the large cooler that Micah had already filled with ice. Once finished, she closed the lid and sat on top of it. Her petite frame barely covered half of the cooler.

"Part of me is always going to love him, Serena," Erika said of Elliott. "He was my first love. And even though Aaron wasn't conceived in the best of circumstances, Elliott is still his father. Every time I kiss my son and look into his beautiful eyes, I see part of Elliott.

"I guess that's what I'm struggling with. If he's really getting married to someone else, then that means there really is no chance for us to make our family work."

Serena turned away from the sink, where she had dumped a bag of frozen jumbo shrimp to thaw.

"E, come on," she said softly. "Didn't that dream die a long time ago? What have the past three years been about?

Playing head games to see how long Elliott would play along? He's been on his best behavior, but do you really believe he's changed?"

"Maybe so," Erika answered softly. "He comes to church just about every Sunday, he plays well with Aaron during their supervised visits, and he's never raised his voice at me since I moved back to Richmond. People do change, you know, Serena."

Both women jumped when the side kitchen door creaked open. Derrick stood there with a pan of just-off-the-grill chicken. His eyes told them he'd heard enough.

"And some people don't," he said calmly. Derrick placed the chicken on the counter near the oven and grabbed a paper towel from the stainless steel holder near Serena.

He rested his hands on Serena's shoulders and kissed her cheek. Sadness swam in his deep brown eyes. "Thanks for having me, lady. I think it's time I get back to Northern Virginia before the holiday weekend traffic on I-95 gets worse."

When he turned to leave, Erika stood and grabbed his arm. "Derrick, wait!"

He paused and studied her.

Tawana, who was watching Jaden, Jacob, and Aaron, yelled for Serena, as if on cue. "I need your help with one of the twins!"

Thank you, Daddy, Serena prayed. She trotted outside, but not before she heard the anger and hurt in Derrick's voice.

"You're using me, Erika."

7

By late afternoon, Serena's worries about the state of her home had been abandoned. Jacob, Jaden, Misha, and Aaron gleefully rotated from the redwood swing set in the backyard to games of hide-and-seek to trying on character costumes and performing for the adults. Misha wasn't self-conscious about being the oldest; she played along and dressed as Dash from *The Incredibles*.

"I don't know why you always turn into Molly Maid just before guests arrive, especially with a houseful of kids," Micah scolded her while they worked together in the kitchen to restock the food for the table outdoors.

She laughed and shrugged. "I have my mother's southern genes. When guests are coming, you prepare."

"What's up with Erika and Derrick?" Micah asked. "They're sitting together, but barely talking."

Serena shook her head. "Long story. I'll fill you in later. I'm just glad he decided to stay."

Ian, Bethany, and their daughter, Victoria, arrived at 4:00 p.m. Sharp.

Serena leveled her eyes at Tawana and Erika, who sat

with her at the picnic table, helping wrap corn in foil for the grill.

"How do they do that?" she whispered. "It's like Bethany has an internal computer that sets itself, to the second, to get her exactly where she needs to be, at exactly the right time. If I'm going anywhere with the boys, I start four hours beforehand and *still* get there thirty minutes late!"

The three ladies laughed.

"That's just it," Erika said. "She doesn't have little kids to worry about. It probably takes her four hours to get herself together, though. Look at her. She could have just stepped off a New York Fashion Week runway."

Ian crossed the lawn to greet Serena and she rose from the bench to hug him. His next target was Micah, who he shooed from the grill so he could take over.

Bethany stopped at a lawn chair near the fence and waved at Serena and her friends. She didn't waste time on pleasantries. "May I have a cloth or wet paper towel? I want to wipe down this lawn chair," she told Serena.

"It should be clean, Bethany," Serena said. "We took them out of the garage just a few hours ago, so they've been sheltered from the elements. I guess you don't plan on using barbecue sauce, huh?"

Serena took in the model-thin former Miss New Jersey's white sleeveless linen top and matching skirt and her three-inch gold and white opened-toed sandals. Every coffee brown spiral curl was in place and perfectly complemented her caramel complexion.

Bethany easily looked a decade younger than her forty-three years, and when she smiled, her face seemed graced with sunshine.

Then she has to open that mouth, Serena thought.

It was clear that Bethany was used to leaving men, and women, awestruck, and her daughter, Victoria, already knew that her startling beauty had the same effect.

The sixteen-year-old glided across the backyard in a tangerine mini-dress and wedge sandals that complemented her shapely legs. The hair that usually fell well below her shoulders was pulled up into a bun, and oversized dark shades covered most of her face, protecting her translucent fair skin from the sun.

Victoria came prepared to decline the chips, hot dogs, soda, and other typical cookout fare. She held up the bag she'd brought along—it contained Perrier and Boca burgers. She sauntered over to Micah, who had agreed to share cooking duties with Ian, and asked the men to grill two of the soy patties, one for her and one for her mother. Then she surveyed the landscape to find the tree with the most shade and planted herself in the lawn chair already positioned there. With the Bluetooth in her ear, she fielded calls from a purple cell phone that spouted a different Beyoncé tune each time it rang.

Serena returned with a hand towel so Bethany could dust the cloth lawn chair. Instead, Bethany placed it on the seat and got comfortable. She pulled a wide-brimmed straw hat and supersized shades out of a designer shoulder bag, then glanced at her daughter and shook her head.

"That child reminds me so much of myself at that age," Bethany said. "Isn't she something else?"

The lack of response didn't faze her. Bethany opened a copy of *Vogue* and flipped through its pages while she waited for her husband to deliver her burger.

Micah cranked up the volume on the CD player he had placed on the patio and picked up his tongs to remove the chicken from the grill. Jazz filled the air, and Ian, who stood nearby basting ribs, bobbed his head to the music.

Serena walked past them and rubbed the back of Micah's neck. "This is what I call keeping it real, bruh."

He grinned, and she knew he, too, was thinking about the surround-sound system they had used often at their Cobblestone Creek house. When Standing Rock Community Church dismissed Micah and he decided to establish a ministry, they sold that house, moved into Serena's childhood home, and went back to basic living without missing a beat. Having Aaron live there with them while Erika got on her feet had made it all the more special.

The birth of their twins had forced Serena and Micah to find more space. They wound up renting Serena's house to Erika.

The little money left in a savings account opened years ago for Serena by her father, Melvin, had been used to put a down payment on this house in one of Richmond's older, tree-lined neighborhoods. The two-story property with a wraparound porch had a full basement and finished walk-up attic but needed renovation and minor repairs, so it hadn't cost a mint like the Cobblestone Creek mini-mansion. Still, Serena and Micah were surviving on Micah's income, so they made do with what they had.

Serena went inside to grab more sodas and walked in on Tawana, who was talking softly to someone on her cell phone.

"I'd like to see you on Tuesday, Grant, but I don't know.

I have my final meeting with my study group, from seven to nine, before most of us leave for the summer."

Serena knew she should cough or somehow let Tawana know she was there, but she didn't.

"Okay, nine thirty will work, but only for a little while." She folded the phone and wiggled her hips.

"You sure all he wants is a date?"

Tawana turned quickly and frowned. "You were eavesdropping."

Serena raised her palms. "I'm sorry, T. I came in for something and overheard you. What's going on with you?"

"Why?"

Serena approached her. "You know why. What's with dating all these different guys?"

Anger flashed in Tawana's eyes. "I see you've been talking to my mother. I know Mama moved up to help me with Misha, but I'm a grown woman. If I can't be at the best university in the nation and enjoy it, what's the point?"

How do I reach her? Serena remained silent.

"I'm not going to be twenty-three forever," Tawana continued. "I need to go out and experience life whenever I can get away from the books. I know, I know—you want to know why I don't go to church too. Aren't you always telling me it's not about sitting in the pews? I still believe in God; I just need to take a break for a minute."

Serena touched her arm. "What if God decided to do that too?" she asked.

Tawana shrugged and brushed past Serena and slid open the door leading to the patio.

"I don't know, Serena. Maybe he already has."

8

Tawana checked her watch and walked faster. It was already 9:20. Grant had agreed to meet her in the parking lot in front of her apartment in ten minutes. She jumped in her car and sped toward home.

She'd had a great time over the weekend in Richmond—all three Carter women had. Mama was rejuvenated from her special time with her sisters and her friend Ms. Brenda. Misha loved having other children to play with, even if they were all boys; and for her part, she had enjoyed hanging out with Serena and Micah and their friends without worrying about an exam or the need to research a particular case. Grant's call had been the icing on the cake.

Despite the lecture from Serena, Tawana had been thrilled by his request to meet her after her study session. He'd been on her mind for the rest of her visit.

Thinking about him kept her from fretting over her new dilemma. With Serena reluctantly preparing for Micah's sister and her two children to visit, she hadn't had the nerve to ask about a twelve-week stay for herself and Misha during the summer.

What was she going to do now?

Grant pulled up alongside her older model Toyota and stepped out of his charcoal gray BMW. He walked briskly toward Tawana and opened her door.

"Hello, beautiful," he said and leaned inside until their faces nearly touched.

She could smell his rich cologne. His smooth lips grazed hers, but she pulled back. When he held out his hand, she clasped it and stepped out of the car. This was how she wanted to be treated.

Grant opened the door to his car and she slid into the passenger seat as if she did this every day. The Eric Benét song floating from the speakers made her smile. That same song had wafted through the window of a slowly passing car when they took an after-dinner stroll on their first date, and Grant had begun singing it to her.

He must have been thinking about me all weekend too, she thought.

"Where to?" he asked once he buckled in.

Tawana shrugged, hoping she wasn't wearing the weariness of a long day on her face. "I'm not picky, but I don't want to stay out too late."

"You still have a curfew?" Grant laughed and covered the stick shift with his hand. He throttled it back, then raced toward the street. "Want Thai, Italian, Jamaican, or American cuisine?"

Now it was Tawana's turn to chuckle. "Talk about giving a lady choices! The last time we had Italian; let's try one of the others."

They settled on 9 Tastes, a Thai spot not far from Harvard Square.

As they waited for their meal to arrive, they continued the get-to-know-you banter they had begun on their first date a few weeks earlier.

"How was your visit home to Richmond this weekend?" Grant asked.

Tawana shrugged.

"Richmond is Richmond," she said. "I guess everyone says that about their hometown, though. It was great to spend time with my friend Serena and her family. How often do you go home to San Francisco?"

"Usually just for the holidays," he said. "Mom and Dad stay busy with their plastic surgery and dermatology practices, and with the hectic schedules of my teenage brother and sister. When I go home outside of Christmas, Thanksgiving, and Easter I barely see them anyway. I have a few relatives on the East Coast and in parts of the Southeast that I visit occasionally, so it's not too bad."

"Knowing all of this and you still want to follow in your dad's footsteps?" Tawana queried.

Grant nodded. "When most people hear 'plastic surgery,' they automatically think about face-lifts and breast implants," he said. "But I grew up hearing my dad talk about the people he helped who had been disfigured in accidents or by birth defects as well. I've always liked the idea of being able to transform someone's life. And it didn't hurt that my dad made a boatload of cash in the process!" He reared back in his seat and smiled. "This type of medicine is a natural fit for me."

Tawana held her breath. They had covered some of the basics on their last date, but she knew tonight he would ask more probing questions about her family and friends. As long as she focused on her years at U.Va., she was in respectable territory. Unless they got serious, no need to bring up Misha, either.

He surprised her, though. Instead of conducting a mock interview that required her to do everything except provide a copy of her birth certificate, he wanted to know more about her vision for her life.

"What are your long-term goals?"

That was an easy one. "I'm going to be the female Johnnie Cochran."

She appreciated that he didn't blow her off or laugh.

"Why'd you decide to study criminal law instead of corporate?"

Tawana couldn't tell him that she'd seen enough of her childhood friends arrested, convicted, and even sentenced to death to run a thriving criminal defense practice in the heart of Richmond. Some of those people probably couldn't be saved, but others had been railroaded.

A good defense could have helped a lot of them, including a few of her cousins. They wouldn't be able to afford the private practice fee she would charge after graduating from Harvard Law, but she could help them.

Instead of sharing all of that, Tawana gave Grant the public relations spiel. "People accused of crimes need excellent representation. Plus, it's a challenge to be the one with the deck stacked against you and you pull off a miracle, sometimes literally, to save your clients' lives."

Grant laughed heartily. "You sound as if you've been practicing for years. What firm are you with?"

Tawana smiled. "You need some representation?"

Grant leaned forward and caressed her hands. "Maybe I do."

It was close to midnight when they left the restaurant, and Tawana tried to put the image of her mother's stern face out of her mind.

Once they settled into Grant's car, he didn't waste any time. "Let me see what that Pad Thai tastes like."

Tawana frowned. "I didn't get a doggy bag."

He smiled and moved close to kiss her.

This time she didn't pull away.

Grant peered into her eyes. "Wanna go back to my place?"

Tawana thought about their last date, when he stood at her door asking a similar question. She lowered her gaze but remained silent. His wallet, on the panel between the seats, caught her eye. Two $100 bills peeked from the corner. Suddenly, she remembered her summer housing dilemma.

Her breath caught in her throat. As quickly as the thought came, she tried to push it away. What would she think of herself afterward? All the times before, it had just been for affection, or to reassure herself that she was desirable.

Grant stroked her cheek and waited, as he had the last time, while she wrestled with the voices in her head.

There was no way she could afford Misha's summer camp fees and rent for an apartment, even a small one, on the internship stipend she'd receive from the law firm. And she certainly wasn't going to stay with either of her aunts. One cursed like a sailor and the other drank one forty-ounce bottle of beer after another, as if she were consuming water. Both of them lived in the housing project Tawana had been desperate to leave when she finished high school.

Misha's much older father had moved on by then, in search of other gullible girls he could have his way with until they wound up pregnant. Tawana knew he had fathered three other children by girls who lived in her neighborhood—a fact he was proud of, but one she cried over, because she knew someday she'd have to tell Misha.

When Serena and Micah had loaded Tawana, her mother, and Misha into the Jeep to take them to Charlottesville for Tawana's freshman year at U.Va., Tawana had looked back only once, just long enough to bid goodbye to a difficult past.

She would do whatever she had to do, to keep from going back there with her child.

Her hands trembling, Tawana reached for Grant's face and kissed him deeply.

"How much is it worth to you?"

9

Serena couldn't figure it out. The house held only four people, now that their guests were gone, and those two boys still had it sounding like headquarters for the neighborhood preschool program.

She rolled over and glanced at the clock. 6:32 a.m. Whether she liked it or not, her day had begun.

Serena rubbed Micah's back, but he didn't stir. Now that leading New Hope Community Ministries was a full-time job, he tried to work from 9:00 a.m. to 7:00 p.m., but on most days he stayed longer.

A corner in the basement of Stillwell Elementary served as his "office"; however, he usually spent his days visiting sick members, testifying in juvenile court, or establishing partnerships between New Hope and community programs that served residents of the neighborhood. When the school day ended, he used the gym to lead Bible study, oversee youth programs, or meet with ministry leaders.

Knowing the weight of his schedule, Serena tried not to begrudge him his rest. Today, though, she was grumpy.

"At least one of us can sleep in," she mumbled, then uttered a prayer: *Lord, please help me adjust my attitude.*

She sat up and stretched to wake herself. If she took any longer, four feet would be pitter-pattering down the hall.

When Jacob and Jaden turned two last December, she and Micah had replaced their cribs with toddler beds. The boys now felt free to roam where they wanted, which forced Serena to keep a portable gate at the top of the stairs.

She scurried to their bedroom this morning and chuckled when she reached the doorway. The Spiderman and Batman sheets and comforters from both beds were in the middle of the floor, and two bumps were visible beneath them.

"If you two little terrors don't get up and get back to bed . . ."

She knew her orders were laughable. They wouldn't be sleepy enough to rest for hours. She crawled on the floor between them and laid on top of the covers, waiting for them to realize she was there. When they did, they scrambled out of hiding and climbed on her back. She tickled them until they giggled with abandon.

Micah can't be sleeping through all of this, she thought at one point. *Sorry, babe!*

By the time Jacob and Jaden had settled down, she was worn out. She stood up and tightened the belt to her robe.

"This is why I start my day out tired," she told the oblivious boys and waved a finger at them. "Help Mommy clean up your room. No breakfast yet. Help clean up!"

Serena made their beds and supervised as they chucked the toys they had strung across the floor into the toy box. She issued her daily warning as the three of them traipsed down the stairs.

"If that room gets destroyed again, Mommy's going to get you . . ."

Micah stood in the door watching as her voice trailed off.

"That's what they want," he called after her. "They're thinking, 'Get me what, Mommy? A toy? Some candy?'"

"Morning, babe," Serena said, ignoring his jibe. *You stay here with them all day then.* "What do you want for breakfast?"

Her day had been reduced to taking breakfast, lunch, and dinner orders; playdates and parties; stay-at-home mothers' group meetings; and stretch jeans or other clothing that she hoped hid her growing assets. Micah said he didn't mind, but she was determined to lose the three pant sizes necessary to fit back into the size 8 jeans tucked in the back of her closet. She had long ago accepted that part of it was vanity, but truth be told, she just felt better when she was fit, and she needed all the energy she could muster to keep up with these twins and Micah's increasingly hectic ministry schedule.

Micah entered the kitchen and rubbed her shoulders.

"Too bad Fric and Frac are up," he said, referring to the boys. "You know what I'd really like this morning."

"Humph, that's how the two of them got here." Given how she had longed to have a baby, she knew Micah took her words in jest.

"And?" he retorted.

While the oatmeal simmered and Micah's coffee began to percolate, Serena dashed outside to grab the newspaper. Maybe while Micah was still home she could get part of it read.

The lead story focused on a missing teen. He left home to hang out with friends, eventually parted ways with them, and hadn't returned.

Serena sat at the table and read parts of the story aloud to Micah while he poured juice for the boys.

"He seems to have disappeared without a trace, but everyone quoted in the story says he's a good kid; he wouldn't do something irresponsible like not calling his parents to check in."

Since her sons' births, any story related to the harm or potential harm of a child sent chills through her. She recalled the day in the grocery store when she'd briefly lost Jaden.

Lord, bring this child home safely. With her eyes open and still fixed on the article, Serena prayed for the missing boy's parents and for police working the case to find him quickly.

Her reverie was broken the second she uttered amen. Jacob and Jaden tore through the kitchen and then back through the dining room, playing what appeared to be a two-year-old version of tag. Or maybe it was just "run fast and hit your brother as hard as you can" time, Serena surmised.

"Stop running! Time to eat!"

She poured Micah a cup of coffee and was reaching for two small bowls for the boys' oatmeal when a thud and scream interrupted her.

"Little boy!"

Jacob had opened the fridge and tried to grab the milk. The half-full gallon jug had fallen on his foot.

Micah, who had been reading the Sports section, dashed to Jacob's side and cradled him on his lap. He bent the boy's toes back and forth while Jacob screamed as if he'd never walk again.

"Nothing's broken, man. It'll feel better in a minute. That was a no-no!"

Serena sighed. Micah didn't have to worry about his medical training going to waste around here. Some of his relatives still questioned why he'd gone through medical school and even a residency before realizing the ministry was his true calling. Serena was convinced that it was because God knew he'd someday be a cash-strapped preacher in need of routine medical knowledge to raise two daredevil boys.

"You sure he's fine?"

Micah nodded and held on to Jacob. He returned to his seat, still holding him. "Get Jaden, love."

Serena, who had pulled out the mop and bucket to clean up the spilled milk, looked up just in time to see Jaden trying to climb up the front of his high chair.

"I get in! I hungry!"

She dropped the mop and dashed over to him. "You can't do that by yourself, Jaden! You know Mommy has to help you!"

She lifted him into her arms and held him there while she removed the tray. Once he slid into the seat, she returned the tray and placed a bowl of warm oatmeal in front of him.

Jacob had spilled most of the milk, but enough had been salvaged for all of them to have a dash of it in their hot cereal.

"Eat, sweetie," Serena said.

She looked at the digital clock on the microwave. 7:12 a.m. Suddenly she wasn't hungry anymore. How was she going to make it another fourteen hours without losing her sanity?

Give me strength, Lord.

On days like this, she questioned whether she was cut out to stay home full time.

With the cost of day care for two babies and the stress of trying to juggle work with their care, her staying home had made the most sense for their family. Plus, she had prayed and longed forever to bring children into the world. When she got pregnant, she had decided to enjoy every minute with them.

Serena still felt that way, but there was also the tug to throw up her hands and crawl into a hole. Some days she felt like asking God if he'd made a mistake. She couldn't be doing this mommy job well by his standards, the way she yelled, got frustrated, and envied her friends who could juggle work and family. She missed talking to other adults and her husband about things other than potty training mishaps, the boys' shenanigans, or the simple but exciting new things they were learning.

Then there were her friends who had given up careers to raise their children and loved every minute of it. They had the patience of Job, kept their houses spotless, and still managed to fit into their size 6 jeans. Which handbook had she failed to read?

And here she was, married to a preacher, supposedly the wife and mother almost everyone else viewed as the standard to model. At New Hope, though, they knew better. During one special service, Jaden had refused to settle down and had cried so loudly that a girl sitting behind Serena with her grandmother stood up and tapped Serena on the shoulder.

"Mrs. McDaniels, why doesn't the baby like church?" The girl, who couldn't have been more than five, waited intently for Serena's answer.

Serena wrestled with the sleepy boy and whispered a reply to the girl. "I'm not sure, Reesa, but I need to figure it out."

Serena's pity parties didn't happen every day, but it was often enough that she had begun praying for God to forgive her and help her get over the "grass is greener" syndrome.

She sat down this morning with a glass of apple juice and tried to quickly skim the rest of the paper while her family ate. A reference on the front of the Metro section to a story inside caught her eye: "Local youth leader cites innovation as reason for success."

Serena turned to page B3 to the photo and lengthy article about Casey Divers, the woman she had trained to fill her shoes nearly three years ago when she resigned from the Children's Art Coalition.

Casey worked with her for six months before assuming the executive director position. She came to the job with other nonprofit leadership experience, unlike Serena, who had career-hopped from the advertising world.

The *Times-Dispatch* article described Casey as a breath

of fresh air, a trendsetter in the nonprofit world, and a legacy maker.

Well, what was I, puffed wheat?

Serena felt ashamed of the knot of jealousy that settled in her stomach. She sighed loudly and slid the article in front of Micah.

He glanced at it and then at her. "So?"

"Nothing. Guess I'm just feeling nostalgic."

Micah shrugged. "That's understandable. But this is a different season right now. The boys need you."

Serena forced a smile. "I know."

Micah resumed reading the Sports section, oblivious to the tinge of sadness in Serena's voice.

Jaden climbed down from his father's lap and toddled over to Serena with a sippy cup in one hand. "Wuv you, Mommy."

Serena wasn't sure why, but suddenly she wanted to cry.

"I love you too, little man."

10

Erika sipped her spiced chai latte and stared at her boss. She was in dangerous territory.

Every professional training program in the history of the world advised against workplace relationships, and here she was sitting with a man who paid her bills *and* made her heart race.

Derrick had come to Richmond this morning to join her and Gabrielle in a series of meetings with local clients. He also had agreed to help her prepare for the National Council for Interior Design exam. But that was before last month, when she had invited him to the cookout at Serena and Micah's. She didn't know now if he was still willing to spend hours with her going over the material. Since the cookout, they had corresponded mostly through Gabrielle or via email.

Today was a D-day of sorts. She had asked him to meet her early this morning, but she wasn't certain whether to stick to business and talk to him later about their personal issues, or vice versa.

Gabrielle had advised her to get the personal out of the

way. "If you don't, it's going to be hanging between the two of you like the pink elephant in the room. Our clients will be able to tell. We don't want them to have any concerns."

So here they sat, in Vie De France, the cozy restaurant located in the James Center atrium, in the heart of Richmond's business district. She tore off a piece of her cinnamon scone and popped it into her mouth.

Derrick glanced at his watch and took a sip of coffee. He settled in the booth and, with his eyes and squared jaw, told Erika he wasn't too happy with her right now.

"You've grown a goatee," she said.

Derrick didn't take the bait. He leaned forward and wrapped his hands around the sides of his cup. "We've got a lot of work to do today, Erika. What do you need to talk to me about?"

She sighed and dabbed her lips with the paper napkin she'd been clutching on her lap. "I don't know, Derrick. A lot of things, I guess. I don't blame you for not returning my calls, but then again, there's too much between us to play these games."

He frowned. "Erika, maybe you need to look in the mirror."

"Excuse me? I've left you several messages apologizing for making you feel 'used' when you came down last month," she said. "It was a knee-jerk reaction to something Elliott did, and I was wrong. I was dead wrong. But I do care about you, Derrick."

He nodded and adjusted his tie. If nothing else, Erika knew he was still hitting the gym most weeknights. The tailored shirt hugged his bulging arms in the right places. She tried to focus on what he was saying.

"You have a funny way of showing it, Erika. If you're still reacting to the antics of your abusive husband, that says a lot. You need to figure out where you stand with him before you'll ever be able to move forward with another relationship.

"We've talked about this before. You and I are always going to be friends. You are an excellent employee. Nothing has changed since I first expressed how I felt about you; I'm here for you no matter what. But it's been two years, Erika."

Derrick slipped on his suit jacket and shrugged it into place. "You. Know. How. I feel. About. You."

A chill coursed through Erika as he punctuated each word. Elliott used to speak to her that way, but his emphasis always dripped with venom. Derrick's conviction conveyed an emotion she wasn't sure she could handle yet.

She tried to keep her voice from trembling.

"I know, Derrick," she whispered. "I'm sorry."

Why couldn't she tell him that she felt the same?

Derrick sat back and sighed. She could tell that he was wrestling with himself too. In his eyes she saw the same emotions jockeying for space inside of her—anger, frustration, and love.

"What is it, Erika? What is the problem?"

When she didn't respond, he continued.

"You know I love God too. I know that God hates divorce. But he also says that a husband is supposed to love his wife in the same way that Christ loved the church."

He leaned forward and lowered his voice. "I'm not trying to compromise your faith or your integrity. I don't want for either of us to be outside of God's will. But I also don't think our Lord wants to keep you in a relationship that could be dangerous for you and for Aaron."

Erika hunched her shoulders and leaned forward too. "That's part of it, Derrick. How do I know that he's still abusive? Elliott says he's changed. Don't I have an obligation, before God, to give him a chance to prove it?"

"If that's what you believe, then why haven't you gone back home?"

Erika sat up straight. The question caught her off guard. Why hadn't she?

"When we're in tune with God, he gives us discernment, Erika. You know that inner voice that we want to call intuition? That's God nudging us to do one thing or another. Something has kept you from reconciling with him.

"You need to figure out what that something is, and I don't want it to be just because of me. You need to make the decision that's going to be best for you and for Aaron, and if you feel like that's staying married to Elliott, then so be it. But I refuse to continue being strung along.

"I love you, but I love myself too. I deserve better."

Erika's eyes widened. "What are you saying? Didn't you just tell me you care about me?"

Derrick cupped her hands in his. Erika was stunned to see tears pool in his eyes.

"I don't just care about you, Erika. I love you. I've known that for a long time." He said it so softly she thought she hadn't heard correctly. But he wasn't finished.

"You're used to a love that hurts; I'm not. If we will ever be together—and that is just a hypothetical *if*, at this point—you've got to learn a better way. Love isn't supposed to hurt. It's supposed to build both people up. Where you and I are now . . . it's tearing both of us down.

"You concentrate on Erika, on loving yourself and figuring out what you want. I am always here for you and for Aaron, even if you decide to stay with Elliott. But for now, we are just friends, and when we're in the office, colleagues. I'm praying for you, Erika."

Erika pulled her hands from Derrick's grasp and wrapped her arms around herself. She thought she might lose it, right then and there.

When Derrick laid fifteen dollars on the table and picked up his briefcase, she realized she already had lost him.

11

Today the tears stopped.

The way her mother looked at her this morning told Tawana if she didn't pull herself together, she'd soon find herself admitted to a local hospital.

"You've been crying for two weeks and you won't tell me why. Misha doesn't hear you every night, but I do. You're losing weight, drinking bottle after bottle of wine, and using all the tissue in the house. What is going on with you, Tawana? Do I need to call a doctor?"

Mama had ranted before, but today she picked up the yellow pages to find some help.

Tawana dashed over and snatched the book from her. "No, Mama! I'm fine; I just have a lot on my mind."

"I can see that, Tawana."

Ms. Carter extended her hand for Tawana to return the the phone book. "Since you won't talk to me, you're going to talk to someone. I didn't come up here with you to this highfalutin' place so this fancy education you're gettin' could drive you crazy. Misha needs you."

She formed a thin line with her lips, but Tawana already

knew what her mother was too proud to admit: *she* needed her too.

Tawana fell to her knees and laid her head on her mother's lap. Sobs wracked her body.

Ms. Carter rubbed her daughter's back and wept too. "What is it, Tawana? What is wrong?"

When the tears finally abated, Tawana sat back and wiped her eyes with the heels of her hands. "I don't want to talk about it, Mama, but I'm going to be okay. I'm sorry I've scared you; it's just been a stressful time. It's going to be alright."

Ms. Carter stared at Tawana, wanting to believe her.

"One of them boyfriends did something to you, didn't he?" She said it quietly, as if she already knew the answer.

Tawana stood and turned away. "I'm okay, Mama. I don't want to talk about it. Everything is going to be fine."

She left Ms. Carter staring at her back and walked to her room where she softly closed the door. She fell across her bed and willed the tears to stop. There was too much at stake for her to allow her world to come crashing down now.

But her mind kept traveling back to the night she had made that split-second decision to sell herself to Grant.

The contempt in his eyes still haunted her. "You want me to pay for it? Look at me, *Tawana*." He had sneered at her and had looked himself up and down. "Do I look like I need to pay somebody to sleep with me? I like to have a good time, but I ain't desperate."

Grant looked at his wallet and saw what had caught her eye.

"You need some money? Here."

He slid the $200 from his wallet and threw it onto her lap.

Tawana, near tears, shook her head and tried to give it back.

Grant pushed the money away and started the car.

Tawana folded the cash and tucked it under his wallet. He pulled out of the restaurant parking lot and headed toward her apartment.

"Are you that strapped for cash?"

She lowered her head and shrugged. "I've never done that before. I . . . I don't know what came over me. I'm worried about a place to stay this summer, and I . . . I don't know. I'm sorry."

Grant took a deep breath and placed his hand over hers. "Don't worry about it."

It should have ended there, with the ultimate humiliation and a strained goodbye.

But she had squeezed his hand and looked at him, wanting him to still like her. "Can we still go back to your place?"

Grant didn't reply, but he steered his car right instead of left at the next intersection.

That night had been different from the others. Her previous suitors had at least whispered sweet lies in her ear and pretended to care. They said all the loving words she wished they meant. She knew they didn't—how could they, after one or two dates? Yet hearing them made her feel good, all the same.

Grant, on the other hand, simply seemed determined to give her what she obviously wanted. She stayed until the wee hours of the morning, allowing him to do and say things to her that let her know he saw her as nothing more than a piece of meat.

It wasn't against her will; she had offered. But after that night, she would never be the same.

When he was finally ready to sleep, he rolled to one side of the bed, away from her. "How did you get into Harvard with a name like *Tawana* anyway? I'll take you back to your car in the morning, 'kay?" He was asleep before she could respond to either question.

The next morning, on the drive to the parking lot adjacent to her apartment, he apologized. "Um, I want you to know that I'm a really nice guy. You said you don't normally do something like that. Well, I try to respect girls too. I guess we were both thinking out of our heads."

He pulled up beside her car and leaned across her to open the passenger door so she could step out. "No hard feelings?"

Tawana didn't look at him. He sped away while she stood there fumbling through her purse for her car keys.

It had been hard to live with herself ever since.

She had crossed a line, and it scared her. Could it happen again? How had she done it so easily? Sleeping with Grant had been insane, but if it had been for pay, she could have been arrested. Before it had begun, her career would have been over.

Those thoughts fueled a fresh round of tears, but Tawana breathed them away.

An India.Arie song floated through her mind. *Get it together . . . Whatsoever you sow you shall reap . . .*

That was one of Serena's favorite songs. Her influence was palpable even when she wasn't around.

In that instant, Tawana knew what she needed to do. She reached across the comforter for the cordless phone and dialed Serena's cell. It was the middle of the afternoon on Saturday, and Tawana knew it was unlikely that she'd be at home.

Serena picked up on the first ring. Tawana could tell she was at a park or in her backyard, because the boys were yelling about kicking and throwing balls.

"I've been waiting to hear from you. Glad you finally called."

"Huh?" Tawana sat up in bed and frowned.

"Your mother called me last week and told me something was wrong. Instead of trying to wring it out of you, I decided to wait for your call. I knew I'd hear from you when you were ready to talk."

"What made you so sure I'd call you?"

"I told you a long time ago that I'm always here for you, T, and you know I meant it. I just prayed that you would remember.

"Whatever's going on, I've got your back. And you-know-who does too."

"God?"

"God."

12

Before she changed her mind, Tawana poured it out. At least most of it.

The date. The sex. The regret.

She waited for the verbal beat down from Serena, but when the prolonged silence continued, she realized Serena was crying.

"Do you hate me?" Tawana asked.

"No, baby," Serena sniffled. "I hurt for you. I want you to stop believing you need to give your body to others to be loved. That's not how it works, T. Why'd you do it?"

Tawana hesitated.

"T?"

Tawana couldn't bring herself to tell Serena she'd initially been after money. She also didn't want to lie. "It's a long story, Serena. Can we skip that part for now?"

Serena usually didn't let her off the hook that easily. Today was no different.

"I'm asking for two reasons," she said. "I want to know only if there's something I can say or do to keep you from going down this road again. But the other reason I asked is because you need to know why you keep doing this, T.

"It's not the first time. You need to figure out why you keep repeating the same mistake. You know I love Misha, but if you aren't careful, you're going to wind up in law school with two babies. Or you just might not finish."

Serena's words felt like a slap in the face. What if she knew the whole truth?

Tawana knew, though, that her friend's questions were valid. If Tawana hadn't been worried about a place to stay, she might not have snapped.

The truth shall set you free.

Tawana sat up and opened her eyes. Where had that come from?

"T, you still there?"

Tawana remembered Serena was on the phone. She could still truthfully answer the question without adding the background details.

"Yeah, I'm here," she paused. "I know you've got a lot going on, Serena, but I need a huge favor."

"Anything."

"Don't you want to know what it is first?" Tawana asked and smiled.

"You're at a place right now where you need to know that you're not alone. Whatever it is, you've got it. Now, it might require some maneuvering with my babies, but I'm there."

Tawana laughed. "You know they aren't babies anymore."

"Back to the subject, Miss Thang. What do you need?"

Tawana went for it. "A place to stay this summer. With Misha. For twelve weeks."

She held her breath and waited for the understandable excuse Serena was about to render.

"The guest room will be ready. Is Ms. Carter going to stay with us too? Why didn't you ask me when you were here for the weekend?"

Relieved, Tawana laid back across the bed. "I'm going to be a summer associate at Wallace, Jones and Johns while I'm there. Misha's already enrolled in a summer camp during the day, and Mama's going to be staying with Ms. Brenda and working in a church nursery for the summer.

"I wanted to ask you that weekend, but then you mentioned that Micah's sister and her kids were coming and what a headache it would be to have more children underfoot. I've been trying to figure out something else so we wouldn't have to bother you."

"Oh, Tawana," Serena said and sighed. "This lets me know that the First Lady has some work to do—on my attitude and my mouth.

"I was just doing my routine griping. I didn't really mean it. I'm glad Evelyn, Zuri, and Tyra are coming; I want to get to know my sister-in-law better. I get overwhelmed sometimes and start ranting, and then I'm okay. I didn't mean for you to take it the wrong way."

"You and Misha are family," Serena said. "It shouldn't have been a second thought, regardless of who comes to visit. If it would be too much for me, I'd tell you, okay? When are you coming and when do you start work?"

Words escaped Tawana. She'd been on the brink of living death. She had crossed a line that could have consumed her soul. Only one thing had saved her.

Grace.

13

Serena ended the call with Tawana and looked across the yard at Jaden and Jacob. Micah was throwing a football and both of them were scrambling to catch it.

She shook her head. They were going to be filthy.

"You've got bath duty, Daddy!" she yelled to Micah. Her gave her a thumbs-up before ordering his sons to get into position.

"Hut! Hut!"

Serena laughed. They didn't have a clue what they were doing. But if their Daddy said run and catch the ball, they were in the game.

"I'm going for a walk," she called to Micah.

The day was warm but cloudy, so a midafternoon stroll shouldn't leave her too uncomfortable. After Tawana's disturbing call, she needed some time alone. With her heavenly Daddy.

She strolled down the sidewalk, past well-kept houses and neat lawns, and replayed the conversation with Tawana in her mind.

She gave me part of the story but not all of it, Serena mused.

Ms. Carter had been frantic with worry when she called. *But you've got this, Daddy. As long as you know what's going on, she'll get through this.*

Serena's thoughts turned to herself, and how her pessimism had affected Tawana's comfort in confiding in her. She remembered her anxiousness over Bethany's visit to her house, and her comments about the bother of having her sister-in-law's children in her space. She recalled her snide remarks about Bethany and Victoria during the cookout.

Serena could recount the times she'd been the brunt of catty conversations herself. As the wife of the senior pastor at Standing Rock, she had been under constant scrutiny, and it hadn't felt good. People at New Hope watched her too, but thankfully this was the kind of ministry that put people on a level playing field. She was respected but not revered, and that was how she liked it.

Now Bethany was another story. That woman craved attention like some women coveted chocolate.

But I've been wrong, Daddy, Serena prayed. *This has nothing to do with Bethany. She's yours to handle. Help me to keep my eyes and my heart focused on you. You've blessed me with so much, Lord, I don't know why I'm having such a hard time appreciating it.*

She smiled and waved at a neighbor and continued walking and praying silently.

People look at me and think they're seeing an example of who you are. That's a scary thought, Lord. I feel so way off track sometimes that I don't even know who I am. I've got the wife part down. Thank you for blessing me with a loving and giving husband, Daddy. And he is fine too. Thank you for that. But everything else? I'm just a mess.

She thought about the recent newspaper article about her former colleague. She had penned a letter of congratulations to Casey, despite a lingering twinge of jealousy. Then there was the house. Even if she had the money to paint, refinish, and refurnish everything she longed to, she wouldn't have the time. The twins consumed so much of her spirit that her brain and her body often felt like mush. And what was she going to do if what she suspected was true? She'd lose her mind.

Do you hear all of this, Daddy? How did I get here?

The answer came quickly. *Be still and know that I am God.*

"I know," she said out loud.

As a woman thinketh, so is she, came the response.

"So now you're telling me I'm a mess because I think I am?"

Serena reached the end of the sixth block and decided to turn around and head back home. She realized if she didn't stop talking aloud, passersby might call mental health authorities.

She understood, though, what Daddy was trying to tell her. If only it were that simple.

Serena reached her house just as the mail carrier was pulling away from her box. She opened it and pulled out a stack of envelopes, magazines, and direct mail fliers.

By the time she entered the house, it was a struggle to remember the conversation she'd just had with God. Micah and the boys were in the kitchen slurping ice cream cones. The TV droned in the background, with an update on that teenage boy who had gone missing two weeks earlier. Apparently he had been found dead. Serena turned it down so the boys wouldn't hear more and then sat next to Micah at the table.

"What kind of walk was that? You look like you're ready to go off on somebody," Micah told her.

She waved a perfumed rose-pink envelope at Micah. "Here's a letter from Bethany. Addressed to you."

She dropped it in front of him, along with the new issue of *Black Visionaries* magazine. The headline and subtitle read, "Ministers on the Move. Congregations light up the faithful in bold new ways."

Three prominent ministers were featured in the cover photo: Bishop T.D. Jakes of Dallas, Eddie Long of Atlanta, and Micah's former assistant pastor at Standing Rock, who had taken the helm after his firing—Jason Lyons of Richmond, Virginia.

Micah sat back in his chair and looked at Serena. He held up Bethany's letter and shrugged. "Who knows?"

He held up the magazine.

"Now I understand how you felt when you read that newspaper article about Casey Divers."

14

Erika checked her watch.

"I love coming to this place, but the lunchtime wait is entirely too long."

Serena sipped her water and nodded. "You know, we never used to say that when we first found this spot. Mister P's was our thang! Now we're old, with 'bills and babies,' as that North Richmond preacher used to say when his services aired on TV and radio."

"You're not talking about Jason Lyons, are you?"

Serena snorted. "Please. Jason is all over the local and national news now since that magazine article hit the newsstands. But no. I'm talking about the pastor of that North Richmond church off Brookland Park Boulevard, the one my mother used to listen to faithfully on the radio when I was growing up."

Erika turned the conversation back to Jason. "Speaking of Micah's former colleague, what do you guys think about how he's blown up, about how Standing Rock has become a national phenomenon?"

Her sister friend shrugged. "It's hard on Micah, just the

way it all went down. He truly believes that God called him to start an inner-city ministry, not to be focused on television and megachurch stardom. But to see Jason and the folks at Standing Rock doing so well makes him doubt himself. He says he's glad to see God's message getting out there; he just prays that the messengers are sincere. Micah's just trying to be faithful where he's planted."

Erika took in Serena's weary smile. "What about you?"

"Me?" Serena said and sighed. "I'm hanging in there. The twins are blessings, but they're driving me up the wall. Tawana and Misha are moving in for the summer in a week, and Micah's sister and her kids will be visiting. And did I mention that I'm pregnant?"

The waitress arrived, as if on cue, with their fried catfish sandwiches, slaw, and fries. She smiled at Serena. "Congratulations," she said and left the table. Since they weren't regulars anymore, she didn't know Serena or Erika like some of the other staff had.

Erika's eyes widened. "Did you just drop a bomb on me like it was nothing?"

Serena continued as if in a daze. "I can't believe I've told you and I haven't told Micah. I think I'm afraid it's another set of twins."

Erika reached for Serena's hand, to nudge her back to the present. "Serena, what is going on?"

Serena looked at her and let the tears spill. "I'm just overwhelmed, E. Miss 'Got It All Together' needs some help right now."

Erika squeezed her hand. She wanted to know more, like a due date and why Serena was so anxious, but now wasn't the time to pry. She had been in a similar place once, one that no words could describe or soothe.

"Consider it done." If she needed to take the twins off Serena's hands, help with housework, or take her out for dinner once a month, she'd do it. "But first you've got to talk to your husband, okay?"

Serena wiped her eyes and nodded. "I will. Maybe I'll do it as soon as I get home. He's watching the boys now." She tried to smile. "You know I love you, right?"

Erika waved her hand dismissively, but her heart warmed. "Go on, with all the mushy talk. Let's eat."

Halfway through their meal and small talk about Erika's looming interior design exam, Serena turned the tables. "Didn't you tell me that Derrick was going to help you prepare for this exam? Why are you taking a class at Commonwealth University instead?"

Erika looked at her watch again. "Class begins in thirty minutes. I've got to find parking and all that. I don't know if I have time to go into it right now."

Serena gave her the look and folded her arms. "I guess you'll be late today."

Erika returned the expression. "You're getting the Cliffs-Notes version. Basically, Derrick has written me off. He told me until I figured out what I want to do regarding my marriage, he's out of the picture."

Serena raised her palms. "You can't blame him, Erika. Derrick is a good man. He's hung in there a long time, waiting for you to decide what you want, with no real commitment to date or anything. What brought this on?"

"That day at your house, at the picnic," Erika said and took a sip of her tea. "That was his final straw."

"But how can you let him go when it looks like your marriage is over anyway? Didn't you say Elliott is getting married?"

Erika nodded. "That's what his last few letters have said."

"So now you're opening them?"

Erika felt the sting of interrogation. "I'm just confused, Serena. If he's changed, maybe we need to try to work things out."

Serena leaned toward her friend. "Erika, I think you and I both need an intervention."

Erika laughed at Serena's mock seriousness.

"I'm joking," Serena continued, "but I'm serious too. You are fantasizing about returning to a man who beat you for years and who has finally told you that he's marrying someone else. You're losing a man who loves you, flaws and all. Look at the pattern here, sis."

Erika dismissed Serena's diagnosis with a toss of her head. "I think Elliott is just bluffing, Serena, to see what I'm going to do. I think he's tired of waiting and he's ready for me to make up my mind. I'm torn."

An ambulance whizzed past and Serena looked out of the restaurant window on to Second Street. She smirked and folded her arms.

"Think again, Erika, and take a look."

Erika, whose back was to the window, turned to see what had caught Serena's eye.

Elliott was walking toward Mister P's at a leisurely pace. He held hands with a tall, voluptuous version of actress Vanessa Williams, who smiled at him with pouty lips and starstruck eyes. He said something that was obviously funny, because she threw back her head and laughed. He leaned toward her and kissed her neck.

Erika's mouth fell open. She watched the scene with mixed emotions. Did this mean she was free? Did she want to be?

15

It was true.

Serena lay across her bed, holding the pregnancy test and raising the thermometer-like white stick to her eyes every few minutes to double check the reading.

She had as much as told Erika she was pregnant yesterday, but she hadn't known for sure. She was five weeks late, so what else could it have been?

Now it was official.

She had given the boys their baths and taken one herself, to relax her tense muscles. Afterward, she decided to pull out the EPT and get it over with. She would finally know for sure whether the signals her body had been giving her were accurate so she could begin to wrap her mind around the reality of it.

The two blue lines said it all. The McDaniels nursery was open for business.

When Micah came home tonight, she would share the news.

Serena held her stomach, which hadn't been flat for

a few years now, and imagined another life growing there.

"God, you have a sense of humor," she whispered. "I take a prayer walk and tell you I need help to get myself together, and this is your response?"

She uttered the words facetiously, knowing full well that when she took that walk yesterday she already was with child. Plus, how dare she have an attitude about getting pregnant when she had struggled for years to conceive. She thought about the miscarriages, the hormone shots, the false hope she had lived with before God had decided to bless her womb naturally with twins.

Tears formed at the miracle of it all. Serena rose from the bed and shivered. It was late May, but their drafty house was often cool in the evenings. She thought about making herself a cup of tea, then remembered that she didn't have decaffeinated.

Think about the baby.

There went her Diet Cokes for the next nine months. The chocolate, she'd have to ration. Right now, socks were the next best option for warming her up quickly.

She opened her drawer but decided she didn't want to wear the thin trouser socks left over from her days in the working world. She rummaged through Micah's drawer and found a thick pair that he wore when he played basketball with Ian or some of the guys from church.

"Perfect."

When Serena pulled the folded socks from the drawer, a sliver of folded white paper floated out and hit the floor.

Where had that come from? Micah's side of the dresser

top was always cluttered with papers, but this had come from the drawer.

Serena knelt to pick it up and was surprised to see a familiar handwriting. Bethany's.

She opened the torn slip of paper quickly.

Her heart raced as she read the cryptic note.

We need to talk. Call me asap. B.

Serena sat on the floor, in a heap, as if the wind had been knocked out of her. This had to be some kind of joke.

Not her Micah. Not with that . . . *diva.*

There had to be a legitimate explanation.

She sat there, wracking her brain, trying to recall if Micah had mentioned something recently about Ian or Victoria or even Bethany asking to talk with him about a matter of faith. Nothing.

Except for the letter that had come in the mail from Bethany last week. She'd meant to ask him what that was about, but had been so distracted by the *Black Visionaries* feature with Jason Lyons that she'd forgotten to bring it up. He hadn't bothered.

The more her imagination danced, the sicker she felt. Serena clutched her stomach and remembered. The test. The baby.

This couldn't be happening. She heard a thud that finally made her get up from the floor. As she rose, she glanced at the clock—9 p.m. and no Micah. Until an hour ago, she wouldn't have thought anything of it. Now, it could mean the worst.

Serena put one foot in front of the other and propelled herself toward the twins' room. She knew the loud bump she had heard was probably Jaden. He fell out of the bed and stayed deep in sleep on occasion—just often enough for her not to be startled. Serena found him as expected and tucked him back in with his favorite bear.

On the way back to her room, images of Bethany paraded before her eyes . . . Bethany in the form-fitting pantsuit she'd worn to church last week, just the second time she had ventured to New Hope. Bethany stopping by a few weeks ago in a tennis outfit that accentuated her long legs, just as Micah pulled into the driveway and a sweaty Serena finished cleaning the flour-covered kitchen from a mess the boys had made. Bethany calling Micah at the church last month when Serena had been in the grocery store hunting for the mischievous Jaden.

Serena sank to her knees at the foot of her bed. She turned her eyes heavenward and let her heart speak to God's.

At times like this, when she was hurting and unsure of herself, she wished she could pick up the phone and commiserate with her mother. It had been seven years since Mama's death, but when the yearning for Mama's unconditional love and wisdom was at its peak, Serena longed for her like she had slipped away just yesterday.

Mama would have understood this crisis without her uttering a word. Mama would have told her how she had made it through the rough spots in her own marriage and how Serena could navigate this nightmare.

But Mama was resting with the Lord, and as Serena had been learning in the years since her passing, she couldn't rely on anyone else's convictions. Her own faith would have to see her through.

16

Tawana folded the last pair of Misha's shorts and tucked them into the drawer. She set a photo of herself, her daughter, and her mother on the dresser that had once belonged to Serena's mother and checked the bed to make sure she had put everything away. The spacious, pale blue room, down the hall from Serena and Micah's and the boys' bedrooms, felt like home now.

She was back in Richmond and she was happy. After all that had transpired in the past month, it had been good to leave the Boston area. Tawana knew she had to return for her final year of law school, but she hoped this time away would prepare her to go back feeling a lot better about herself and ready to focus on the right things. Whenever she spent time with Serena and Micah, that seemed to happen.

And maybe this time she'd be able to give something back to her friend. When she wasn't working, she could help out with the twins or with a project around the house. She could see that Serena was struggling, but Tawana knew that came with the territory of being a perfectionist, a trait that she, too, had trouble managing.

This summer clerkship was an awesome opportunity to show her skills, learn new ones, and find a mentor with insight into the criminal defense profession. She had already decided that she was going to be the star among the summer associates, whatever it took. She'd begin that journey in three days, and she couldn't wait.

Tawana heard Misha's bubbly laughter floating on the wind. She went over to the window that overlooked the backyard and saw Micah pushing her daughter higher and higher in one of the swings. The boys sat nearby on the swing set, seesawing as fast as they could. Misha looked her way and waved. Tawana returned the gesture and searched for Serena, then remembered that she was in the kitchen putting away the turkey sausage spaghetti, one of her quick-turnaround staple meals that also happened to be Misha's favorite "Aunt Serena dish."

The girl had been ecstatic when Tawana told her they would be spending the summer in Richmond, at her god-parents' home. Ms. Carter had settled in with Ms. Brenda and promised to call and come by often.

Misha's days would be full. After a six-week stint in a creative arts program in the city's West End, the soon-to-be third grader would enroll in a North Richmond camp near Serena's home that emphasized physical fitness and academic skill building.

Tawana marveled at how she was a student paying for these experiences for her daughter when, as a child, she'd never been exposed to them herself. Ms. Carter hadn't even known such programs existed.

When she learned that her law firm stipend was going to be slightly more than she had expected, Tawana decided to give Serena and Micah something modest for rent and groceries. They had insisted that their home was hers and that she save her money for critical needs. However, she wanted to pull her own weight, especially since the Mc-Daniels were living on a single income. Even with paying them, she would be able to cover camp costs and save for Misha's back-to-school expenses.

Serena's sons were young enough that visits to area parks and the Children's Museum were all it took to excite them. She had offered to watch Misha as well, but Tawana knew her daughter would quickly grow bored and become a handful.

Still, Misha couldn't believe how lucky she was to be spending the summer with Jacob and Jaden, the two little brothers she had "always wanted."

"If you have to work all the time as usual, that's okay, Mommy," Misha had told Tawana over dinner earlier tonight, soon after they arrived. "I have to help Aunt Serena with Jake and JayJay, so I won't miss you as much."

Tawana, Serena, and Micah had laughed heartily at her grown-up offer, especially at how in a matter of hours she'd decided that the boys needed nicknames.

Yet Misha's pronouncement had also reverberated within Tawana. She hadn't forgotten Serena's advice from a few months earlier, that Misha needed some special time with her. Tawana planned to make that happen; she just wasn't sure it would be before she finished law school.

○

Downstairs in the kitchen, Serena also watched the children and Micah at play while she washed the dishes from dinner. Just a few hours into their stay, Serena knew it was going to be a joy having a little girl in the house.

She glanced at her purse on a nearby counter and thought about that slip of paper tucked inside, with Bethany's alluring message to Micah. Tawana had offered to babysit tonight so she and Micah could go out for dessert or a movie. She had something more important in mind.

Whatever he said to her after she confronted him, she had made up her mind. As she soaked her hands in the suds, listened to the children's glorious laughter, and thought about the child growing in her womb, Serena readied herself for battle.

17

For the fifth time in the past half hour, Erika dialed the numbers to Elliott's cell phone. As she had done the previous four times, she clicked the off button before pressing the final digit.

What would she say to him? Why was she calling, anyway?

Seeing him last week with the woman at Mister P's had been a wake-up call. Like Derrick, he too had obviously grown tired of waiting for her. Elliott and the mystery woman had strolled past the restaurant that day without seeing Erika or Serena and had entered another Jackson Ward eatery.

Erika had wanted to follow them to watch but restrained herself. She just couldn't believe it. After all of these years, Elliott Wilson had finally moved on? Then why had he continued to string her along, with the cards and calls and requests for dates? Why hadn't he released her so she could move forward with her life too?

When did he ever think about you?

As quickly as that thought surfaced, she ignored it.

Aaron ran into the room, spotted her on the sofa surrounded by textbooks, and crawled into her lap. He rubbed the sleep from his eyes and laid his head on her chest.

"Hi, Mommy. What time is it?"

Her little old man.

"Hi, sweetie." She kissed the top of his head and hugged him. "Did you have a good nap? It was about time for you to wake up."

His midday Saturday snooze had given her an opportunity to study for the prep class for her fast-approaching interior design exam, but she'd wasted a good chunk of time holding the phone.

She glanced at the digital clock on the DVD player. It was just three o'clock. Serena's half sister, Kami, had agreed to come by at four to babysit so Erika could run to the grocery store and complete a few other errands. At least that was what she'd told the girl.

What she really wanted was to talk to Elliott face-to-face, to make peace with his decision so she could figure out God's plan for her life.

Love doesn't hurt.

She recalled her last in-depth conversation with Derrick, and his almond brown face filled her mind. She tried not to think about the way he looked at her, as if his eyes were boring into her soul.

Wonder what he's doing right now?

She pushed the thought away and fanned the bare fingers of her left hand out in front of her. She had long ago stopped wearing the stunning diamond Elliott gave her when they married, but why couldn't she remove his invisible hold?

Erika gazed at Aaron, who snuggled next to her and closed his eyes again. All that she had once loved about her husband was wrapped up in her arms, in this small package.

The dimpled left cheek, the big brown eyes, the smile that turned up at one corner the same as Elliott's.

She was still holding the phone when it rang. She peeked at the Caller ID and picked up on the first ring.

"Hi, Ms. Gregory," she said and smiled, as if Charlotte could see her. "How are you?"

When Erika had finally moved out of Naomi's Nest, she had taken the most special things with her: a worn pair of pink slippers to always remind her of what she had endured and survived while living in the D.C. shelter; the phone number and address of her roommate, Kathy; and Charlotte Gregory's heart.

Charlotte had been the assistant director and Bible study leader at Naomi's Nest for longer than she could remember. She served as a mother figure to many of the young women who sought safety there, but she and Erika had formed a special bond. Charlotte often teased Erika by reminding her that God worked that way.

"He knew you needed a mother, and I guess my four children weren't handful enough for me," she'd say jokingly. "He decided I needed a petite little thing named Erika that I could pick up and put in my pocket!"

Charlotte made her laugh, but she also held her when she cried. She had taught Erika to pray, and to believe that she could become an interior designer if she wanted it badly enough. Charlotte had been by her side helping her push Aaron into the world.

Now that Erika had settled in Richmond, the two of them didn't talk as frequently. But it was like the mother-daughter relationship Erika had always longed to have with her birth mother, one that they could pick up with a phone call or face-to-face meeting as if they'd never been apart.

They chatted for a few minutes before Charlotte announced that she'd been promoted to director of Naomi's Nest.

"Audrey is retiring at the end of the month. They're having a farewell bash for her and a congratulatory reception for me on the same night. You have to come."

Erika promised to be there. She put Aaron on the phone to say hello to Aunt Charlotte, who shared godmother duties with Serena. After he had filled her in on his week at preschool and the latest excitement with his pet fish, he dashed off to his room to play with his trucks.

"I'll get you a snack in a few minutes," Erika called after him before returning her attention to Charlotte. They were chatting about who else was coming to the shelter party when Erika's phone beeped. Her eyes widened when she checked the Caller ID panel and saw Elliott's home number, the one that had once been hers too.

"Charlotte, I'm sorry. Can I put you on hold?"

Erika pressed the Flash button and feigned ignorance. "Hello?"

"Hi there." Elliott's silky smooth tenor caressed the words as if he were singing them.

Erika forced herself to sound nonchalant. "Hi, what's up?"

"Just wanted to chat with you about the request I made a few weeks ago, you know, about the divorce?"

Erika's breath caught in her throat. He was serious. "Hold on a minute, Elliott. Let me get someone off the other line."

She clicked back over to Charlotte. "I've got to take this call from Elliott, Charlotte, but I'll call you back in a little bit."

"Everything okay?"

"He wants a divorce."

"Is that surprising?"

Erika sighed. "I don't know; I guess I'm a little confused. I'll call you back so we can talk about it."

"Okay, baby," Charlotte said soothingly. "Just don't do anything foolish. People can say all the things they think you want to hear, but that doesn't mean they're being honest. Remember that, and be careful."

Erika's mind was already back on Elliott and what this complication meant. She bade Charlotte goodbye and promised to call her in a few days.

"I got your note about getting remarried," she told Elliott a few seconds later.

When he didn't respond, she continued.

"Who is she? When did this come about?"

Elliott chuckled. Erika pictured him sitting at the kitchen table grinning and stroking his chin. She knew he was eating this up, and she was playing right along.

"Why don't we discuss this in person, Erika? Wouldn't that be better, given all that's gone on between us?"

Funny how they were on the same page about meeting. Erika looked at the clock. Kami would arrive in another twenty minutes.

She wasn't crazy enough to invite him into her home, but she had to talk to him, to figure this all out.

They agreed upon a time and place and ended their call.

Erika was rifling through her closet, searching for an appropriate outfit, when it struck her that Elliott hadn't bothered to ask about their son. He hadn't seen or spoken to Aaron since their last supervised visit two weeks earlier. He didn't know that the boy was recovering from a virus or that he was sad because his best friend was moving away.

Erika selected a dress and tried to dismiss a troubling question: Did Elliott care about his son, or was Aaron just another avenue to get close to her?

18

Serena and Micah strolled the path that snaked along the James River.

The night was clear and stars blanketed the sky. Somehow they always found themselves at Brown's Island, at the place where their journey together had begun.

They drew near the restaurant where Micah had proposed seven years ago, and he grabbed her hand. He pulled it to his lips and kissed her palm.

"I love you as much as I did when I asked, you know?"

Serena thought about the paper in her purse that bore Bethany's cryptic message and did not respond.

The restaurant would be open until 1:00 a.m., but it wasn't crowded tonight. Serena was glad. She wanted to talk to her husband as privately as possible.

When the waitress offered them a table for two in the center of the dining area, Serena requested a booth. Micah shrugged and followed.

He ordered Diet Cokes with lemon for both of them, but Serena stopped the waitress before she turned to leave. "Can you bring me water with lemon instead?"

Micah looked around frantically, as if searching for something. "Who are you? Where did Serena go?"

She gave him a wry smile but remained silent. She wanted to get the necessities out of the way before launching into what she really had on her mind.

"Want to split a dessert or order separately so we can try two different ones?" she asked.

"Let's do that," Micah said, referring to the latter.

He chose a towering goblet of apple pie, and she, of course, opted for something with chocolate, fudge, and ice cream. When the food arrived, they traded thoughts about the movie they'd just seen and fed each other bites of the other's selection.

To look at us, no one would guess this might be the end of our marriage as we've known it, Serena thought.

But this was the first time they had been out in months without the children, and despite herself she was enjoying it.

I am the potter, you are the clay.

Serena took the hint. She should know better by now than to go trying to forecast the future.

"It's 10:30. You think Tawana has the boys in bed?"

Serena took a bite of pie and nodded. "Oh, yeah. She's a pro. It was nice of her to give us a date night."

Micah smiled. "Maybe that will happen more often this summer, with her and Misha around. They're good kids."

Serena laughed. "Don't let Tawana hear you call her a kid. Those are fighting words to a woman who's also a mother and a bright law school student."

Micah sat back and wiped his mouth. He pushed the

goblet of pie toward Serena. "You want the rest of this monster? Go for it."

Serena shook her head and pushed hers away too. "It's not like I need any of it."

Micah studied her. "What's on your mind? You've been pretty quiet."

Serena looked at him and sighed. Where should she start? "A lot."

She pulled out the note she'd found in his sock drawer earlier in the week and slid it across the table.

"What is this?" she asked.

Micah concentrated on the paper.

"And this?" She had found the letter Bethany mailed two weeks ago in the trash. It hadn't contained anything explicit, but again, Bethany had requested to see him.

Micah looked at his wife and shook his head. "It is what it is, Serena. I'm not going to lie."

Her heart skipped a beat. Was he going to admit it that easily?

"You need to speak plain English to me, Micah," she said slowly. "I'm not understanding."

He put his elbows on the table and leaned forward. "Yes, Bethany is flirting with me. She was crazy enough to send this letter through the mail, and she stuck that scrap of paper in my pocket at our cookout last month."

"And you didn't tell me? You held on to it?" Serena didn't try to hide her anger.

"To be honest, I thought I'd thrown both of them away."

Lord, please don't let me act a fool in here.

Serena mustered every ounce of restraint she possessed

to keep from smacking her husband across his pensive face.

"Talk to me, Micah."

He locked eyes with his wife. "I don't know what's racing through your mind right now, Serena, but I meant every word I said to you before we walked into this restaurant. I love *you*. Yes, Bethany is beautiful, but so are you. You are the mother of my children and nothing she does can make me stop loving you."

Tears filled her eyes. Serena wanted to believe him so badly. But how many cheating men used similar speeches on their desperate wives? Even preachers?

What had Deacon Melvin Gates told his wife about his affair with her mother all those years ago? The fact that he was Serena's father hadn't been acknowledged until she graduated from college, but Serena knew that the disconnect in both of her parents' marriages had begun at a juncture similar to this point in her relationship. Serena wasn't having it.

"Micah, you know who you are dealing with," she said calmly. "You know my family's history. I'm not Melvin's wife nor my mother. I don't have time for games from you or Bethany. I need you to respect our marriage and tell me what's going on."

Micah sighed. "I'm not a professional therapist, sworn by law to keep a client's confidentiality, but as a minister, I have a similar policy of ethics with people I counsel. You know that."

Serena interrupted him. "So Bethany's been coming to visit you under the pretense of needing counseling?"

Micah shook his head. He looked uncomfortable. "No,

Serena, she hasn't. But she has sent more than these two notes, asking to meet with me. The first time I did meet with her, at a local Starbucks, because she said she wanted to plan a surprise birthday party for Ian."

Serena rolled her eyes. "Miss Socialite needs you to help her plan a party like Donald Trump needs me to manage his assets."

Micah nodded. "Exactly. But that has been the premise under which she keeps sending these notes. I've ignored them.

"The one I've been counseling is Ian. All those hours on the golf course haven't just been for pleasure. He and Bethany are in trouble. He's torn about what to do, and she's scrambling however she can to keep him under her control."

Serena exhaled. She wouldn't have to murder the father of her children after all. "She thinks by flirting with you, Ian will get nervous and start paying attention to her?"

Micah shrugged. "For all I know, she's serious with her advances, Serena. But Ian and I go way back. If I were going to be stupid enough to step out on you, I don't think I'd kill my marriage and one of my deepest friend-ships too."

His hesitation let Serena know he didn't know how much more to say, how much of Ian's confidences to break.

"Look, Bethany's got issues that you wouldn't believe. She's wrapped in a pretty package and she acts as if she's better than everyone else on earth, but underneath all that glitz and glamour are things she doesn't want you or anybody else to know. Ian is trying to be a good husband and father. I'll just leave it at that."

Serena squeezed his hands. "I'm glad you are trying to do right by your friend, Micah. But I have to tell you, when I saw those notes, I was scared."

He frowned. "Do you really think I'd do something like that to us, Serena, after all we've been through together?"

She looked squarely at her husband. Micah had never given her a reason to doubt him, but he was human. He was a man of God, but he was still a *man*. "She *is* gorgeous Micah, and she's not overweight or always distracted by two busy little boys. And those notes were pretty bold."

"You know her, love. She's a bold person. If nothing else, we need to pray for her."

Serena sat back. "That's good and fine. I'll ask God to give me the strength to do that. But you also need to tell her to back off, Micah. I'm not having her disrespecting my house like this. If you don't want to tell her, I will."

Her voice softened. "And I need you to understand that the way you've handled this hasn't been the best for our relationship. I remember you telling me when you entered the ministry that one of your mentors advised you to put God first, family second, and then ministerial duties. I know Ian is your best friend, but you shouldn't be keeping me in the dark about anything that could come between us, not even for him."

Micah gazed out of the window at the river. He was silent for a long time, and when he finally stirred and looked at her, Serena could tell he had been praying.

"No weapon formed against us shall prosper, Serena," he said. "Don't ever think I would hurt you like that, you hear me?"

She was startled by his solemnness.

"I haven't said anything because with everything else going on, I didn't want Ian to know that Bethany was going behind his back doing this too," Micah said. "But I get it—I've got to do what's best for us. And I will."

The knot of tension in Serena's chest unfurled. Preacher or not, Micah wasn't perfect. But as she watched him tonight and listened to him, her heart and her spirit told her he was still the Micah she knew. He was telling her the truth.

She had shared her fears with her father last night, and he advised her with the wisdom of firsthand experience.

"This will be difficult, Serena, but don't turn your ears off to protect your heart," Melvin said. "If you're really listening, and praying for clarity, you'll know whether Micah's feeding you a line or being authentic. Althea knew; your mother's husband knew; and yet they chose to turn the other way rather than confront us.

"I'm not blaming them—your mother and I decided to sin against God and have an affair," he said. "But Herman Jasper and my wife knew that your mother and I didn't need as much time as we took each Sunday to count the weekly offering. Althea told me so years later. She stayed with me and let things run their course because we had a young family."

Serena had sat on her bed with the light off, listening to Melvin. How had he known she needed to hear from him? How had he found the courage to have this conversation with the daughter he had once denied?

He offered to talk to Micah, man to man, if she felt comfortable.

"For now, though, take care of yourself," Melvin advised. "Tell Micah how you feel. Tell him to check this lady and to do what he needs to do to honor your marriage."

Serena had chuckled. "How about get home early enough to handle bathtime more often?"

Melvin's voice rumbled with laughter. "That's 'new school' stuff, daughter," he said. "I can't help you with that. But I *can* tell you that your husband loves you; he's just focused in one direction right now. You know men can't multitask."

Tonight, over dessert, Serena was glad for that. She looked into Micah's eyes and didn't doubt what they revealed. *Cast your burdens on me. I will give you rest. And Ian too.*

God's whisper reassured her. Then Serena giggled.

Micah looked surprised.

"I am so glad I don't have to clean my house anymore when Miss Diva comes over. I've been delivered!"

Micah laughed with her and slid out of his booth.

"Where are you going?"

Before she had completed the question, he was seated next to her, with his hand on her thigh.

He leaned into her and kissed her lips.

"Reverend McDaniels, we are in a public place," Serena whispered. "Some of your church members could be in here; this isn't appropriate."

Micah looked around at the sparsely populated restaurant. The few people there seemed engrossed in their conversations and food.

"I'm wearing a ring and so are you," Micah said mischievously. "Let them watch and see how exciting marriage can be."

He kissed her again.

Serena smiled. She had no idea how she was going to manage in the coming months, but if they were in this together, she would survive.

"Slow down, babe. I'm already pregnant."

19

Erika decided she had lost her mind.

When Kami arrived to babysit, she asked the girl to watch Aaron for most of the evening. With college just months away, Kami was building a stash for miscellaneous spending as quickly as she could. She'd been unable to work much during her senior year of high school; so today she readily agreed and joined Aaron on the sofa to watch *Brother Bear*.

Two hours later, Erika was sitting in Lemaire in the Jefferson Hotel, perusing the menu.

How did I let Elliott talk me into this? she asked herself.

You wanted to come.

Erika wished she had an off and on switch to that inner voice sometimes. She was learning that God's guidance was gentle, yet unrelenting once one invited a relationship with him. Instead of balking, she decided to listen.

Show me what I need to know, Lord. Show me whether to stay or go.

Not that she really had options now that Elliott had a fiancée. Still, she had come prepared to remind him of what he was losing. Why? She was still trying to figure that out.

The elegant black dress she wore accentuated her slender frame, and every piece of her close-cropped hair was in place. The diamond studs in her ears sparkled and her makeup was flawless. The double takes from men at nearby tables told her she'd scored a victory.

Elliott returned from the men's room and found her still considering what to order. "Decided yet?"

"It doesn't matter. Filet mignon will be fine."

"You sure? We haven't eaten out together in a long time. This is special. Let me order for you."

A chill went up Erika's spine. Some things hadn't changed. She wound up with butternut squash bisque and crusted filet of ahi tuna.

She tried to ignore the knot forming in her stomach. "Why did you want to meet with me? To hand over the divorce papers?"

Elliott seemed surprised that she had broached the subject. Erika asked so she could gauge his reaction.

"I do have them with me, yes. But this is the first time in the two years I've been asking that you've agreed to go out with me. I thought I'd take you to what used to be one of our favorite spots, for old times' sake."

Erika frowned but didn't respond.

This used to be his favorite spot. Not hers.

"Clearly you haven't been missing me for the entire two years," she said. "When are you getting married?"

Elliott shrugged. "Mara's thinking about a Christmas wedding, but I'd like for it to be sooner, if you and I can settle our business before then."

Mara. So that was her name.

Erika remembered how he had talked her out of having a wedding. They had eloped to Jamaica instead, so he could attend a law firm conference with his "wife" in tow, prepping him for partnership in the firm.

Sure enough, it had worked. He became partner within the first year of their marriage. They were the postcard pretty couple in public, but at home, Elliott's pretense melted like ice sizzling on a hot stove.

He reached for her hand, and Erika hesitated.

Here's your chance to know whether you still feel something, she told herself.

When she rested her petite palm in his larger one, he spread it open and weaved his fingers through hers.

Erika held her breath.

"You know," he said softly, "we were beautiful together. If you would give us another chance, we could be again. Aaron needs us."

The waitress arrived with their soup and Erika pulled away.

That was her problem: she wanted to believe the fairy tale too. But this was for real; she couldn't just change the channel or pause the movie when things got ugly. Black eyes and bruised ribs hurt.

"Weren't we just talking about your wedding plans to someone else, Elliott? And besides, how could I ever trust you again? You treated me worse than some people treat stray animals."

Elliott gave her a puzzled look. "Erika, I've apologized for my behavior over and over again. I've gone to anger management counseling. I've become a faithful Christian.

I accept only supervised visits with our son. What else do you want me to do?"

He stared at her, waiting for her to answer.

Erika looked deeply into his eyes, as if she could detect deception there. She'd never been able to do it when they were together, so why she believed she had that ability now eluded her.

Because you have me, now.

Ah, that was right. But was that enough? Could God really help her discern someone else's intent or see into his soul?

Charlotte's wisdom played through her mind too: "Anybody can talk a good game. The truth comes out when they're put to the test. That's when you find out whether their talk and their walk line up."

She considered Elliott's question, the one he'd been asking for quite some time now. What did she want him to do? Was there anything he *could* do to make her want to give their marriage another try?

Instead of answering, she played dodge ball, as usual. "I'll ask you again, Elliott. Why are we here when . . . what's her name? Mara, is somewhere waiting to marry you?

"What are you going to do? Break it off with her and move Aaron and me back into your place? If you can cast her aside so easily, do you really love her?"

"Of course I love her. She's a beautiful woman, inside and out." Elliott smiled proudly, as if he deserved no less. Then he leaned toward her again.

"But you were my first love, Erika, and the Bible that you and I live by clearly says to love and honor the wife of your youth. No one is more beautiful to me than you.

You'll always have a special place in my heart. Always. The fact that you are the mother of my son, my firstborn, is even more meaningful."

Erika's heart softened. Part of her would always love him too. It wasn't the desperate love or the thrilling love she'd once felt when she saw him enter a room or heard his name or feared what life would be like without him.

But she was older now, so maybe that made a difference. It was simply . . . familiar. And how awesome was it that, in their own way, each of them had connected with God? She relaxed and decided to enjoy this fancy meal.

"You're good with words, Counselor Wilson."

"I can be a good husband too."

She reminded herself that Elliott was a lawyer. He could banter with the best of them.

They ate mostly in silence, with Elliott gazing at her and she playing over and over in her mind what life would be like if being with him were her reality again.

After the meal, as they waited in valet parking for their vehicles, Erika stood next to Elliott with an ease she hadn't felt in a long time, if ever, really. She wasn't any closer to a decision about whether to move forward with a relationship with him or grant the divorce he had requested. Then again, after tonight, she wasn't sure he still wanted it.

Elliott bent over to kiss her and she backed away.

"Moving fast, aren't we?" she asked nervously.

"We are married, aren't we?"

When she didn't respond, he pulled a slate gray envelope out of the inner pocket of his suit jacket.

"Here are the papers. Take them and read them and let me know what you decide. I meant everything I said tonight. If you will remain my wife, I will do everything in my power to make you and our son happy, Erika. The minute you let me know you want to start over, I will call Mara and tell her we're finished."

The power he had placed in her hands was intoxicating.

Before she could form a response, the parking attendant pulled up and held the door open to her five-year-old Lexus sedan. She waved goodbye and drove away.

As she slowly rounded the curve, she saw Elliott say something and slap palms with the attendant who had delivered her car. Another attendant arrived with Elliott's Mercedes. He stuck his hands in his pockets and strutted to the vehicle with a smile. All these years later, little had changed in his self-assured swagger.

Thoughts of Derrick invaded the moment.

20

Serena knew the instant she awoke that God had especially kissed this day. She couldn't pinpoint any particular reason, but she felt it with a knowing that defied explanation.

Maybe it was the lightness in her spirit after her heart-to-heart talk with Micah last night. She fell asleep in his arms with a peace that had eluded her in recent days.

She went to dinner last night prepared to tell him that now wasn't the time to start wavering on his vows, but that hadn't been necessary. He had been smart enough to take her to the place that reminded her why she had married him. There, she could be as honest with him as she had been when they had their very first lunch and became instant friends. There, instead of thinking about the dirty laundry he scattered on the floor or the household repairs that remained undone, she remembered all the times she had needed him to stand with her, or for her, or to love her in spite of her shortcomings, and how Micah had never let her down.

Or maybe her joy this morning was related to having

Tawana and Misha under their roof. Their presence had already added a warmth to the household, as if the old Colonial functioned better with more people, connected to each other, underfoot.

Serena wasn't sure what about this day was speaking to her, but she uttered an extra-special prayer of thanks before lifting her head from her pillow.

She stretched and looked at the digital clock on her bedside, surprised that the twins hadn't served as her alarm. Seven thirty was late for them to still be asleep. Tawana had allowed them to stay up until just after nine, though, with an apology about a movie delaying bath time.

Serena had understood. They were going to be a handful to settle down at bedtime for a while until they got used to having Misha around. This morning, Serena was grateful for the reprieve.

She rolled over to greet her husband with a kiss and found his side of the bed empty. Ah, Sunday morning prayer. He had made his way to his attic-level study.

Serena nearly jumped out of her skin when she descended the stairs and heard the clang and clatter of pots. Then she remembered Tawana.

"Good morning, Goldilocks," Serena said as she entered the kitchen, clutching her chest. "You almost gave me a heart attack."

Tawana turned from the stove where she was flipping pancakes. "Goldilocks?"

"Yeah, as in 'The Three Bears.' I didn't know who was up in my porridge."

The two women laughed until tears almost rolled.

Serena started a pot of coffee for Micah. He never ate

before he preached, but she usually got him to consume something liquid.

She turned on the small TV attached to one of the cabinets and channel surfed, clicking past two prominent local ministers, the Rev. Garland Greer on channel 8 and the Rev. Ulysses Hawthorne of First Baptist on NBC 12. She paused when a commercial featuring Pastor Jason Lyons caught her eye. The PGU Network was now airing Standing Rock services at 8:00 a.m. and again on Sunday evenings.

Tawana turned to look. "He is a good-looking man. And he can preach."

Serena didn't respond. She scanned the faces in the choir behind him and recognized some of her former friends, the ones who saw her in Ukrop's or at one of the area malls and averted their eyes.

Micah came up behind her and rubbed her stomach. "Mornin', love."

Serena looked up at him and smiled. They had decided to keep the baby news to themselves for a while. She grabbed the remote to turn the channel.

Micah waved his hand and sat at the table. "Don't worry about it. You can't live in Richmond and avoid Jason and Standing Rock. They are doing their thing."

Tawana looked at Micah curiously. "How does that make you feel?"

Serena brought him a cup of coffee and sat across from him. She thought she knew the answer but wanted to hear it firsthand.

Micah looked heavenward and then at Tawana. "I'm not going to lie to you. Some days I'll be listening to the radio or I'll pass a Standing Rock billboard and I will ask myself, what was I thinking? Something says to me, 'That could be you on the cover of *Black Visionaries*, driving the Hummer, living large out in Short Pump. You lost your mind.'"

Serena raised her eyebrows in surprise. Micah took a sip of the plain, black coffee and continued.

"That's what I call my bad angel."

He laughed and looked at Serena. He reached over and tenderly stroked her cheek. "Then God scolds me. He reminds me what he was speaking to *my* spirit three years ago. Not once during my prayer time did he nudge me to say yes to PGU or to give in to the demands of Standing Rock's deacon and trustee board and focus on prosperity gospel."

Micah shrugged. "We all know that God works in ways we don't understand. At least I know it. I can speculate all day about why I was fired and why this ministry is thriving under Jason. I just believe that God's Word is true: What God has for me is for me, and that everything happens as it should, even when I don't understand.

"We have more than a thousand members now, and they've blessed me with a full-time livable salary, thank God."

He sighed heavily. "But, we're still meeting at Stillwell Elementary School for services. I can only have 'office hours' with church members when school is over and the administrators have cleared the premises. Things could be a lot more comfortable. Every time I start to feel sorry for myself or question whether I'm successful, somebody will share with me how a New Hope ministry, one of my sermons, or one of our members helped them, and I'm grateful again for where God has planted me."

Micah got up to pour himself another cup of coffee. "Guess you ladies got your sermon already today, huh?"

The three of them laughed.

Tawana flipped the last pancake on top of a large stack and put the platter in the oven to keep them warm. She brought plates of pancakes, eggs, and bacon to the table for herself and Serena and apologized to Micah.

"I didn't realize you fast before your sermons. There are plenty if you want brunch after service."

Micah chuckled. "Don't sweat it. Go ahead and eat. I'm used to Serena and the kids wolfing down food in front of me."

Serena feigned an attitude before she took a bite. "Excuse me?"

Micah winked at her and looked at Tawana. "Thanks for getting up early this morning to cook, T, but don't feel like you've got to be the nanny around here. You're family; you don't have to earn your keep."

Serena nodded in agreement as she consumed the delicious meal. He had spoken before she could.

She picked up the remote and flipped the channels, this time stopping when she saw a breaking news banner on channel 6. She turned up the volume.

The weekend anchor was reporting the latest regarding the search for suspects in the murder of the teen whose disappearance and tragic discovery had been the top local news story for weeks. The community had been on pins and needles, worried sick that other youths in their quiet suburban area might be at risk. But the anchor announced this morning that a suspect was now in custody.

"Eighteen-year-old Neal Lewis, the son of prominent

banker Walker Lewis, has been charged with first-degree murder for the slaying of Drew Thomas. Neal Lewis is a recent graduate of the prestigious Seward School in Washington, D.C., and is slated to enroll in Stanford University in the fall. Sources close to the case say that Neal Lewis was a frequent visitor to Richmond and that he and the victim met at a party earlier this year at a mutual friend's Richmond home. No motive has been released at this time, but late yesterday, the young suspect's parents retained the services of Wallace, Jones and Johns, the nationally respected criminal defense firm based here in Richmond."

Micah and Serena looked at Tawana.

"That's your firm," Serena said.

With her eyes still glued to the tube, Tawana nodded.

"Looks like I'm not going to have much time for cooking after today anyway."

21

Serena arrived at Stillwell Elementary School for New Hope's 9:00 a.m. service and got a possible inkling of why she had awakened this morning with such conviction. God was going to make her a more patient woman today—her limits were already being tested.

The classrooms in the third grade wing of the school had flooded during a heavy overnight rain, so there would be no nursery care today. It was every parent for himself or herself. Besides that wing of the school, the only other areas of the building Micah had permission to use were the gym, where members worshipped, and the cafeteria, which the ministry used as a fellowship hall.

Mr. Bracey, the school's janitor, arrived just after 8:30 a.m. so he could dry and clean the three affected classrooms for the students and teacher who would need them tomorrow.

"None of the books or desks were damaged, but how many times are they going to let this happen before they do something?" he grumbled. "If this hallway didn't slope down, the standing water in here could have flowed in the other direction and messed up the gym floor."

He shook his head and pushed his glasses up on the bridge of his small nose. "The last week of school and the kids have to come back to this mess tomorrow. I told the bigwigs around here a long time ago that a good storm was going to flood these classrooms. This wing of the building sits lower than the rest of the school, and when it was added on, it wasn't constructed well. Plus, it's just plain old. I've been complaining about water seepage and leaks in the roof for years, but don't nobody listen to me."

Serena smiled and patted his arm. She was glad he cared so much about the students and the school. "I'm guessing a lack of money is partly to blame, Mr. Bracey," she said. "Since you're already here, are you going to stay for service?"

He clutched the vacuum hose that he would use in a few minutes to suction the water before he mopped. "I guess I could, First Lady McDaniels."

Serena didn't argue with his formality. She knew Mr. Bracey's generation didn't play when it came to respecting their church leaders.

"Good," Serena said. "Feel free to sit with me, but don't worry about my being offended if you choose not to. Since the nursery's closed, I'm going to have my hands full."

She pointed down the hallway at the twins, who were running in circles around Tawana, with Misha right behind them. "They slept later than usual this morning, but I'm hoping they'll still fall asleep in church."

Micah rounded the corner and approached just in time to respond. He shook Mr. Bracey's hand and playfully nudged

Serena. "Sorry, lady. I'm not that type of preacher. My sermons leave even the babies spellbound."

Serena rolled her eyes. "How about I let them run wild just as you're getting into your message?"

Instead of teasing her further, he nodded toward the door. Serena turned and waved when she saw Erika enter, with Aaron trotting behind her. Micah touched Serena's shoulder.

"Gotta run and get ready. Looks like you'll have lots of help with the boys, love. I'll keep the service short and sweet—for all of you parents who've lost your quiet time today."

Serena narrowed her eyes and shook her fist at him. She turned and hugged Mr. Bracey. "See you in the gym, Mr. B. Let me round up my little fellas."

He returned to his work, and to his grumbling.

Serena approached her friends and lifted Aaron in the air for a hug. "How's my little man?"

"Hi, Auntie," he said and squeezed her neck tight enough that his miniature muscles bulged through his blue collared shirt.

Aaron may not have remembered living with Serena and Micah from six weeks old until just after his first birthday, but his affection for the couple remained tender. He had been the first baby Serena had nurtured and bonded with, during a period she had believed she would never bear children of her own. Aaron had shown her what it meant to love someone more than herself and as much as she loved her spouse. He would always be part of her, as much as her twins and the baby growing inside of her now.

Serena lowered him to the ground so he could join Misha

and the boys in a game of uncoordinated patty-cake. She leaned toward Erika to kiss her cheek. Midway there, she saw her friend's eyes.

"What's wrong?" she asked softly.

"Elliott is here, with his . . . fiancée."

Tawana and Serena strained their necks to see, but they were the only ones in the long hallway.

"They just pulled up in his car," Erika said. "I don't believe him."

Serena frowned. "Why do you care? Isn't that a good thing? Maybe now he'll leave you alone and you can get on with your life."

And with Derrick, Serena wanted to say, but thought better of it. She knew Erika well enough to know something had happened between her and Elliott. Erika's refusal to elaborate simply confirmed it.

"You're playing with fire, girl," Serena said. "I don't care how much Elliott comes to church, sends you thoughtful cards, or spouts the pretty words you long to hear, you need to be careful. If nothing else, ask yourself why he's wooing you but prancing around here with another woman on his arm. That alone should tell you he ain't about nothing."

Erika shrugged. "It's not easy to end a marriage Serena, especially when a child is involved."

Serena saw her watching the door, waiting for him to enter.

"He's been really good with Aaron, and he hasn't harmed me or threatened me since I've moved back to Richmond. Anybody can change, with God's help," Erika said.

Tawana listened, wide-eyed. "Do you still love him, Erika?"

Erika looked from Tawana to Serena.

"Everybody's not going to have a relationship as perfect as yours and Micah's, Serena," Erika responded. "Sometimes you have to make the best of life, based on the choices you've already made."

Serena put a hand on her hip and furrowed her brow. She wasn't going to let Erika deflect the attention from herself. "Erika, come on. You've been back in Richmond for more than two years, and you're trying to tell me that all of a sudden you've decided your marriage is worth saving?"

Erika didn't respond, so Serena continued.

"And who said my life was perfect? Or my marriage? We have our ups and downs just like everybody else. Our glue is the word Tawana just mentioned—*love*.

"I love Micah enough to stand with him through thick and thin, to deny myself something if it will make his life better. I have no doubt that he's there for me in the same way. Can you say that about Elliott? What are you afraid of, Erika?"

Erika turned away from Serena and sighed.

The choir launched into a morning worship song, and Tawana began rounding up the kids.

Help her, Lord. Serena uttered a prayer for Erika that she had prayed years ago, when she realized during their college days that Elliott was regularly beating her. She knew by now, though, that she couldn't preach common sense into her friend. The difference this time was that Erika had her own relationship with God. That alone reassured Serena.

If she won't talk to me, Daddy, please let her hear and follow you.

Serena led the group into the gym, where she chose a section of empty chairs about four rows from the front. She went all the way to the end so she wouldn't have to climb over anyone if she had to remove one or both of her restless sons from the service. It was reassuring to look throughout the seats and see other mothers making similar strategic moves or pulling out crackers, cookies, and juice to keep their little ones happy.

She sat one son on either side of her and handed each of them crayons and Bible coloring books to keep them occupied, at least briefly, before she stood to join in the choir's song of praise. She swayed and clapped to the music, until Tawana, who sat next to one of the twins, tugged at her skirt and motioned with her head to look toward the front.

While Serena had been engrossed in worship, Ian, Bethany, and Victoria had filed into cushioned folding chairs on the second row. Bethany sat on the end closest to Micah's floor-level podium, looking like an attentive wife supporting her husband. She waved and smiled at Micah, who acknowledged Ian with a nod instead.

As the song ended and everyone settled into their seats to open their Bibles, Serena struggled to keep her composure.

Remember why you're here, she told herself. *To worship God, to enter into his presence.*

She already knew what was coming after the service, however. She looked at Micah, and his eyes told her he was ready.

Bethany had gone too far. It was on.

22

Tawana pulled into the parking lot behind the Wallace, Jones and Johns suite of offices and walked the few steps from her car to the entrance. She rang the buzzer next to the tinted glass door and waited under the veranda for Emery Goodwin to usher her in.

Because of all of the media coverage surrounding the Neal Lewis case, Ms. Goodwin had called Tawana on Sunday evening and instructed her to arrive at 7:00 a.m. instead of 9:00, and to be sure to come to the rear of the building. No media were in sight this early on a Monday, but that didn't mean they weren't lurking nearby.

Someone peeked out of the corner of the drapery and opened the door. "Come in quickly."

Tawana entered and shook hands with Ms. Goodwin, who had sounded older on the phone than the late thirties or early forties she appeared to be.

"Please call me Emery," she said. "It's nice to meet you after having talked with you by telephone so many times. Welcome to Wallace, Jones and Johns. Two other summer associates should be here momentarily, and then I'll take the three of you in to meet the partners."

Brandon and Heather had rented units in the same apartment complex and were riding together this morning, Emery said.

Ten minutes later, they joined Tawana and Emery in the firm's small cafeteria and introduced themselves.

"Brandon Robinson, Temple."

"Heather Sherman, Stanford."

Suddenly the shame from her overnight date with Grant came rushing back. She remembered how he had uttered her name with such disdain. *Tawana.* The two associates waited expectantly.

"I'm . . . T. Elise Carter. Harvard."

Emery looked at Tawana quizzically. "I've been calling you by the wrong name all this time?"

Tawana laughed nervously and shook her head.

"No, no. You've been using my legal first name, but my middle name is Elise and I typically go by that." She shrank inside as she told the white lie. Elise was her middle name, but she had never really cared for it or felt the need to use it, before now.

Emery peered over her thick black glasses at Tawana but didn't share her thoughts. "Okay."

She ushered the law students into the large conference room, where the three partners for which the firm was named sat at the head of a massive mahogany table. Six full-time associate lawyers flanked their bosses. Each had been scribbling notes before Brandon, Heather, and Tawana entered.

Bob Wallace motioned for the new law clerks to join them at the twenty-seat table.

"Welcome aboard, ladies and gentleman." His booming voice and the sweeping gesture he made with his hands reminded Tawana of a circus ringmaster. She, Heather, and Brandon looked at one another out of the corners of their eyes but tried to focus.

"I'm sure you've watched the news," he continued. "We are front and center in the city's most high-profile case of the summer. Neal Lewis is a bright young man with a bright future that . . . guess what?"

He raised his arms as if directing a choir.

"Rests in our hands," he said, finishing his thought. "That means all hands are on deck!" He pointed to Tawana, Brandon, and Heather. "That means you three are going to be in the trenches with the rest of the firm. You are on our team and you're going to learn how a blue-chip criminal defense firm wins its cases!"

Ken Jones stood and introduced himself next. In stark contrast to Bob Wallace's pomp and circumstance manner, he spoke slowly and deliberately.

"Welcome aboard," he said. "Bob's right. This is a small firm, but we do excellent work, and we do it by focusing as a team. Each of you was handpicked to work here this summer. That means you're up to the challenge, and as Bob said, we have a big one before us. This case will probably garner national attention, so be prepared for intense scrutiny, along with long hours."

Vincent Johns summed it up, from the comfort of his seat, where he pulled his tie slowly askew while he talked. "My partners have said everything we usually cover with summer hires. I'll just add that we're glad to have you here, and if you have questions, please don't be afraid to ask.

Yes, we'll be under the gun with this case, but we know you're still learning. Don't assume anything. Please. If you don't know or if you aren't sure, ask."

The staff attorneys introduced themselves before the three law students took their turns again. This time Tawana's middle name rolled off her tongue more smoothly.

"I'm T. Elise Carter. Please call me Elise. I'm a rising third-year student at Harvard, and I'm looking forward to being part of the team."

Twelve hours later, when she returned to Serena's house with a briefcase full of notes that detailed what the firm knew of Neal Lewis's whereabouts in the week before, during, and after Drew Thomas's disappearance, Tawana's head was spinning.

Misha met her at the door and hugged her waist tightly. "I had so much fun at camp, Mommy! We colored and painted and made music . . ."

As Misha recounted her day, Tawana looked at Serena, who was dabbing Neosporin on Jacob's scraped knee, and mouthed "Thanks." Serena had picked Misha up from camp and fed her dinner. If the summer was going to be as intense and grueling as today, Tawana realized she might be relying on her friend more than she had anticipated.

She just hoped it wouldn't be a burden.

23

"Hello. D. Haven Interior Design. Derrick speaking."

Hearing his voice made her realize how much she missed him. It was after five on a Friday. Erika had expected his voice mail to pick up, although she still would have likely stumbled over her words.

"Hi."

"Hello?" Derrick obviously hadn't heard her.

She said it louder. "Hi."

This time he seemed puzzled. "Yes?"

"It's me, Derrick. Erika."

His silence made her wonder what he was thinking.

"How are you doing?" she asked.

"I'm fine, Erika. Heading out the door. What's up?"

Weeks had passed since their morning meeting in Richmond, and they had been handling business-related correspondence through Gabrielle. Today, however, Erika needed to talk to him herself. She hadn't forgotten the number to his private line.

"I wanted to say hello. And let you know I passed the exam."

"That is great news, Erika. Great news. Congratulations." His voice softened, and she could tell his enthusiasm was sincere. "How does it feel?"

She smiled and held the cell phone closer to her ear. "The day of the exam? I was terrified. When the results arrived in the mail today, elated. You're the first person I called."

He didn't respond.

"So . . . what have you been up to?" She wanted to kick herself for not being able to think of something more clever.

"I should be asking you that, Erika."

She heard the strain in his voice and knew he was wondering whether she had made a decision. Derrick wasn't one to play along. He had told her where they stood, and he wasn't going to get caught in the middle.

But she didn't want to talk about Elliott right now. This was her moment with him. "I'm still praying about what to do, Derrick."

His short laugh almost sounded like a bark. Erika heard the hurt.

"God does answer, you know," he said. "We have to be listening."

Someone must have entered his office. Derrick covered the phone so that his words were muffled. She couldn't hear what was said or to whom he was speaking.

"Hey, that's great news about the exam," he said when he returned his attention to Erika. "I'm proud of you. I've got to run. Have a good weekend."

With that, he was gone.

Erika laid the cell phone on the bed next to the pile of mail and wept.

God, is this what you want me to do? Ignore how I feel about him?

She had planned to ask Derrick to meet her next week when she traveled to D.C. for Charlotte's promotion celebration. His response just now had been her answer. She covered her mouth with her hand so that Aaron, who was watching cartoons in the next room, wouldn't hear her sobbing and come running.

She wanted to believe that her heart wouldn't lead her wrong, but hadn't it taken her down a dangerous path the first time, with Elliott? This time, she was determined to use her head. She also intended to do it God's way, and everything she read during her personal study time told her to be patient and long-suffering, to yield to what God wanted, not her own desires.

Aaron needed his father, especially if Elliott had become a better man. And the Scriptures she studied stated unequivocally that God hated divorce. If she followed her head and the Holy Word, surely she would get it right.

Even if "right" means love slips away?

Erika ignored that voice and wiped her eyes with the back of her hand. She shuffled through the rest of the mail, knowing she would find it there as usual. A card from Elliott. How she wished the return address were Derrick's. She ripped it open and read the note her estranged husband had scribbled this time.

I'm waiting. For you.

She thought about the devotion on obedience, sacrifice, and God's unconditional love she had read this morning.

Erika wished there were a hotline to heaven, a number she could dial that would give her a road map for her life. Wasn't the Good Book supposed to serve that purpose? Maybe she needed to talk to Reverend Micah, because clearly she wasn't reading the right passages.

24

Would. Could. Should.

Serena tossed those words around her mind like salad as she stretched out on the sofa and watched *The View*. It wasn't the same without Star Jones, but oh well.

She would get up and fold the laundry, but her body was dog tired.

She could get dinner started, since Melvin had picked up the boys and taken them back to his house to visit with Althea and Kami, but she didn't feel like rummaging through the freezer to figure out what to cook.

She should be reading one of the dozen or so books stacked next to her bed like a paper mountain, but that would require more brain cells than she felt like expending.

Instead, she lay here feeling frumpy and full, having just eaten a bag of popcorn and a bowl of low-fat chocolate ice cream for her midmorning snack. She knew better.

Serena smiled to herself and rubbed her belly. Mama would have told her she deserved a day to veg out—popcorn, ice cream, TV, dirty clothes, and all. The thought made her relax. By the time *The View* was running credits, she had dozed off.

Her eyes flew open at the insistent ringing of the door-bell. Serena sat up and glanced at the wall clock. It was noon. She had slept for half an hour.

Was Kami or Melvin bringing Jacob and Jaden home already? She doubted that, since Althea had taken the day off work to hang out with them. She didn't expect to see them until later this evening, just in time for bed.

Serena stiffly stood up and walked toward the front door. She hadn't suffered morning sickness this time around, but her spreading hips burned as if she were training for a mara-thon. She and Micah still weren't sharing their news, but if anyone looked closely, they'd either figure it out or attribute her growing abdomen to too many high-carb dinners.

Serena peeped through one of the glass panes in the front door. Who else would show up without calling first but Bethany?

Serena considered tiptoeing away, but she knew Miss Diva had seen her. After their run-in at church on Sunday, she was surprised at Bethany's nerve.

She didn't take me seriously. I guess I need to tell her again. God help me to keep you in this conversation.

Serena opened the door and waited. In her skin-tight citrus capris, off-the-shoulder belted top, dangling over-sized hoop earrings, and jewel-studded wedge sandals, Bethany looked gorgeous.

A month ago, Serena would have taken one look at her and shriveled inside. Today, she felt free in a pair of Micah's faded jeans and one of his Commonwealth Uni-versity T-shirts.

"Yes?" she finally said.

"Did I wake you, Serena? You look . . ." Bethany's voice trailed off when she read the warning in Serena's eyes. "May I come in? I think we need to talk about what happened on Sunday. It's all a big misunderstanding."

She waited expectantly, but Serena didn't move.

The fruit of the Spirit is patience, kindness, peace, self-control, love . . .

Serena sighed. *Do I have to be nice to her?*

The answer came swiftly. *She's one of my children, too, whether she knows it or not.*

Serena opened the door wider so Bethany could enter. She closed it behind her and led Bethany to the living room, the one place guaranteed to be spotless, no matter what chaos reigned in the rest of the house.

She pointed Bethany to the plush burgundy chair near the window and sat in the matching one adjacent to it. She could tell that Bethany felt uncomfortable but wasn't sure if it was because of the formality of the room or because of what she had come to say.

Serena usually ushered Bethany into the kitchen, but her efforts to forge a friendship were over. Her mother taught her long ago that she could befriend anybody, but that didn't mean everybody belonged in her inner circle. Bethany had come close, because of Ian, but now that she had crossed the line, it would be a gift if Serena politely referred to her as an acquaintance.

"Serena, I stopped by to apologize."

"For?"

Bethany shrugged and looked down. "On Sunday you accused me of repeatedly flirting with Micah, even while we were in church. I'm sorry if I've done anything to make you feel threatened. I was sitting there right next to Ian. Why would I do that? My husband takes good care of me and Victoria. We have a beautiful home, we take dream vacations, we have a good life."

Bethany's eyes darted around as she talked. Serena reclined in her chair and watched.

"Would Ian agree with you?"

The question caught Bethany off guard. "What does Ian have to do with this?"

Serena sat up in her chair. "Ian has everything to do with it. He's the one giving you the lifestyle you've bragged about. He's the one who bought that fabulous outfit you're wearing. He's the one trying to get closer to God while you're in church making eyes at another man, who just happens to be his best friend and also a minister showing him the true source of life."

Serena hadn't turned any pages in her stack of novels upstairs, but she could tell by Bethany's reaction that she had read this woman like a book.

"The biggest problem with all of this is the woman that Ian's 'best friend' just happens to be married to—me."

Bethany squirmed in her seat and frowned. "Where is all of this anger coming from? I thought you were supposed to be so Christian."

Serena narrowed her eyes. "I love God with all my heart, Bethany. He has blessed my life in too many ways for me to name, and one of those gifts is Micah McDaniels.

"God loves me when I'm right, he forgives me when I'm wrong, and he's working on me constantly so that I'll do the same with others, including you. But I'm telling you right now that whatever you're doing to destroy your family, you need to keep mine out of it.

"Any woman who is bold enough to send a letter to another man, knowing that his wife is home all day and checks the mail, is looking for trouble. Well, guess what, lady? You found it."

Bethany's eyes clouded over in dismay. She rose from the seat, pressed her fingers to her lips, and walked briskly toward the door. Before Serena could lift herself from her sitting position, she heard it close behind Bethany.

"Good riddance," she said aloud.

But Serena didn't feel giddy as she had expected. Just because she could remove Bethany from her life didn't mean Ian could extricate himself as easily, or that he even wanted to. And there was Victoria. Serena prayed that the girl wouldn't emulate her mother's practice of securing validation in things or in people she considered a challenge to draw into her web.

If anything, Serena felt sad that a woman so physically beautiful was tearing down everything around her that really mattered. The people closest to her would be left behind to clean up the mess.

25

Tawana sat across from Arlen Edwards and Bridgette Hayes and tried to swallow the lump in her throat. Her first summer clerkship and here she sat in the middle of one of the biggest cases of the year.

She had been paired with the two Wallace, Jones and Johns staff lawyers to help with research, interviews, and other legwork in preparation for Neal Lewis's fast-approaching arraignment for murder. Brandon and Heather were working on parts of the case with the other four staff attorneys.

This morning Tawana, Arlen, and Bridgette had come to the city lockup to meet Neal and ask him more questions about his recent visits to Richmond.

The firm's partners had interviewed Neal and his parents twice but wanted the others on the team to know and be comfortable with the person whose life they were trying to save.

"He's a handsome, articulate, very smart kid," Bob Wallace had boomed in the staff briefing yesterday. "That may be the problem. If he comes across as too privileged or too well bred next to his solidly middle-class student body president victim, we may have an image problem that could translate into a guilty verdict. Try to dig up anything you can to humanize him."

At eighteen, Neal was just five years younger than Tawana. Would he take her seriously?

"Just follow my lead with the questioning, okay?" Arlen apparently had noticed her trepidation. She tried to relax.

Bridgette, who was jotting notes about the day of Drew Thomas's disappearance, looked up from her work and glared at Tawana. "Just listen and don't say anything if you're nervous."

Bridgette returned her attention to her notes, and her gray and blond hair fell forward and shielded her eyes. Arlen and Tawana traded looks. He shook his head, indicating that Tawana shouldn't be intimidated.

Neal shuffled in a few minutes later, wearing the standard orange jumpsuit given to inmates. Unlike many young defendants charged with crimes, he had not been allowed to post bail because he was considered a flight risk.

Tawana could see that living in conditions so drastically different from what he was used to already was taking its toll. His green eyes seemed lifeless, and the auburn hair that he had worn almost shoulder length in his senior year picture had been cut short. Today it was matted on one side of his head, as if he hadn't bothered with a comb. He also looked thinner than he had appeared when Tawana saw him for the first time in TV news reports two weeks ago.

The deputy removed the handcuffs from Neal's wrists and pulled out a chair for him next to Arlen. He sat facing Tawana and Bridgette.

When the guard was gone, Neal shook their hands. The lawyers asked him how he was faring and whether the firm could do anything to make him more comfortable.

"If you can get me out of here and keep me from going someplace worse, that will be good enough," he said.

Bridgette got right to business.

"Let's retrace your steps on the night of May fifth," she said. "You told Mr. Wallace you drove down for a party at a friend's guest house. Who was the friend and how many people were at the party?"

Neal sat back and shrugged. "I already shared this with Mr. Wallace and Mr. Johns. Do I have to tell you again?"

Arlen looked him in the eyes. "The prosecutor may ask that very question over and over, twenty different ways, until he wears you down and you say something that leaves a question or a smidgen of doubt about your innocence in the jurors' minds. Get used to us asking the same things, in the same way or different ways. Your story has to be airtight before we can adequately defend you. We've got to know it in our sleep, and so do you."

Tawana's stomach flipped. His story? Wasn't this supposed to be about the truth, about what really happened?

Neal nodded, and Bridgette picked up her pen again.

"My friend was a girl that I met last spring in D.C. She came up from Richmond to a party thrown by a group of girls who attended Seward with me.

"We exchanged numbers . . . and a few kisses." Neal mustered a smile. "She invited me to a pool party she was having in May, and I promised her I'd be there."

"Did your parents know you were coming?" Arlen asked.

"Sort of."

"Be more specific," Bridgette said.

"I told them I was coming to Richmond with my best friend, Steele, to visit his cousin. I didn't tell them it was for a party, and I didn't tell them whose party it was."

"Why not?" Tawana knew the question was simple, but at least she had chimed in.

Neal looked from her to Arlen to Bridgette and hesitated. "Mr. Wallace didn't ask that question," he finally responded.

"Sounds like it needs to be answered, son," Bridgette said. She leaned forward and looked at him intently.

"It's a long story, too complicated to get into, and besides, it has nothing to do with the trial."

The lawyers exchanged glances.

"This is no time for games," Arlen told Neal. "If you don't come clean now, you could wind up losing everything, including your life."

Tawana wasn't sure Neal believed him, but she'd studied enough cases to know Arlen wasn't bluffing.

26

Erika looked to her right and caught a glimpse of the car tucked just beneath the Interstate 95 overpass when she whizzed by.

"Oops."

She eased off of the gas pedal and peered in the rearview mirror. Serena knew her friend was praying that the state trooper hadn't decided to trail her with flashing lights.

Erika glanced at her in the passenger seat and then quickly behind her at Tawana and Kami.

"Guess I better watch this lead foot. Thanks for taking this road trip with me, ladies. I know it took some maneuvering of your schedules, but it means a lot."

Kami piped up first. "Thanks for inviting me. I can't believe my parents let me go away for the weekend by myself, before they were forced to release me to Hampton."

Erika laughed. "Release? That's an interesting choice of word."

Kami nodded. "'Release.' If they had their way, I'd be getting my degree right here in Richmond, at Union University or Commonwealth University, so they could conveniently be in the area to spy on me. HU isn't that far; I wouldn't put it past them to show up on campus pretending to be 'nontraditional students,' so they can reprimand me if I'm having too much fun."

The three older women laughed.

"I felt the same way when I headed off to U.Va.," Tawana said and waved her arms in the air. "I thought I was finally free to do my own thing."

Erika shook her head. "You two babies just don't know how good you've got it. Enjoy this time in school. It's one of the best careers you'll ever have. When you get old like me . . . whew!"

Serena turned in her seat so she could face her half sister.

"Erika's right, baby girl. The next four years are going to be some of the best of your life. I told Melvin he had to let you come with me this weekend. Before I know it, you'll be traveling to D.C. or New York with your college buddies, and you won't have time for your married-with-kids older sister."

Serena once believed she would never accept Melvin Gates as her father, especially since she had grown up without him acknowledging their bond. Time changed things, though. A few years ago he had told Althea and his children about Serena and had asked them to accept her. With her being her mother's only child, Serena realized she would have been an adult orphan if Melvin and his family hadn't embraced her.

It hadn't been easy. Melvin's sons, James and Perrin, remained aloof. Yet Serena had managed to form a deep friendship with her father and his sweet-spirited wife.

She had become a doting big sister to Kami, the couple's youngest child whom she had once envied for her hold on Melvin's heart. Now Kami was eighteen, in love with her high school sweetheart, and preparing to become a psychologist.

When Erika had called Serena last weekend sounding blue, their lengthy conversation had ended with Erika suggesting that her visit to D.C. for Charlotte's party become a sister-friend trip. Erika told Serena to invite Tawana, and Serena had asked if there was room for Kami.

"She needs to know she has a circle of support before she heads off to college," Serena told Erika. "She's been sheltered by Melvin and Althea, but everybody likes to experience life themselves. Maybe some of the advice we share with her on the way to D.C. and during our short visit will seep in."

This afternoon, they cruised along the interstate as if none of them had worries—and for this trip, they didn't. Tawana's mother had come to Serena's home for the weekend to care for Misha, Aaron, and the twins, freeing up Micah to prepare for weekend services. The kids were excited to be doted on by Ms. Carter; the mothers were excited to have some time to themselves.

Erika cranked up the music and sang along to Anthony Hamilton's latest release for a while, and then Janet Jackson's. She smiled sheepishly at Serena.

"I don't listen to gospel artists twenty-four/seven, but the Lord still loves me."

Serena smirked. "Girl, please. I had Micah dancing to some of the same grooves last week when you were kind enough to take the kids for the afternoon."

They all giggled, imagining their baritone-voiced spiritual leader moving to "Sista Big Bones" or "Call On Me."

"Now don't wind up—" Erika stopped herself midsentence. She stole a glance at Serena and issued a silent apology for almost spilling the beans about the pregnancy. Serena winked.

"Watch yourself now," Serena quipped and pointed to Kami. "We have innocent ears in the car."

Serena changed the subject. "Look at us, four fine women jamming our way to the nation's capital. If we weren't women of God, this could be a scene straight out of that old Queen Latifah and Jada Pinkett—before she added the Smith—movie."

Erika lowered the volume of the music. "You mean *Set It Off*? When they played bank robbers?"

Serena nodded. "Play along now. I *said* if we weren't godly women."

Tawana and Kami looked at each other and frowned.

"Y'all are old," Kami said. "I have no idea what you're talking about."

Tawana leaned over and patted Kami's head. "You were still in elementary school when it came out. I think I was about twelve. I saw the previews, but I don't think I ever got to see the movie."

Serena shook her head. "We might be old, but you two have missed some good stuff. We have an assignment when we get back to Richmond—a visit to the video store to check out a classic. Well, that might be overstating it. But the movie is definitely the African American version of *Thelma and Louise* with a couple of extra sisters thrown in for good measure. You've got to see it."

Serena turned up the volume of the music and glanced at the digital time on the dashboard clock, noting that it was just after noon. Ms. Carter was probably preparing the kids' lunch and wondering whether the pay they were offering was enough for the romper room she had agreed to monitor. Micah would be in and out to help, but he usually spent Saturday afternoon preparing for Sunday services.

Right now, though, he was probably still in the backyard with Ian, where Serena had left them building a tree house for the boys. She knew they were also continuing their counseling sessions. Serena secretly questioned whether their talks were helping.

Hurt had spilled from Ian's eyes into his posture that Sunday after church two weeks ago when Micah and Serena had talked with Bethany about her actions. Though Bethany had emphatically denied being flirtatious and had explained away her letters and notes to Micah by referring to the surprise party she was planning for Ian, none of them had bought her story. After forcing Bethany to apologize to Micah and Serena, Ian had taken her by the elbow and led her to their car. Serena wasn't sure what he'd said to Micah later, but whenever Ian saw her, he gave her an extra-tight hug.

God, please bless him. And help him.

Amid all the fun in the car, she uttered the prayer that had become her regular refrain when she thought about Ian. She knew Micah had been praying with and for his friend as well, but she hoped Ian was learning to talk to God for himself.

At some point, and maybe very soon, relying on Micah's faith wasn't going to be enough. Serena couldn't pinpoint why—she just knew.

27

The ninety-minute drive from Richmond to D.C. whizzed by as Serena, Erika, Tawana, and Kami laughed, sang, and reveled in each other's company.

Serena tried to remember the last time she'd felt this lighthearted. By the looks of it, Erika and Tawana were asking themselves the same question. They had needed this getaway.

They strutted off the elevator like runway models when they reached the twenty-first floor of the northwest D.C. building that housed Charlotte's condo.

Charlotte enveloped each of them in heartfelt hugs. Dressed in her trademark blue jean overalls, her salt-and-pepper braids were pulled up into a bun, and her nails were manicured and polished a subtle red. For the first time since Erika had met her, Charlotte's round cheeks shimmered with a touch of blush, and she wore bronze eye shadow that made her eyes dazzle.

"You look absolutely beautiful," Erika said. "But please tell me you aren't going to wear those strapless sandals with these overalls?"

Charlotte swatted at Erika and laughed self-consciously. She pointed toward the bedroom. "My daughters have been over here all day, conducting a *What Not to Wear* session in my closet. Geri went out and bought me an outfit from Nordstrom's. So no, tonight these trusty denims will be staying home. The heels? Who knows?"

Geri and Tanya emerged from the bedroom and pointed at their mother. "What do you ladies think?"

Erika was stunned by how gorgeous Charlotte looked. The makeup accentuated her features, and she simply glowed.

"Who knew she was hiding all this?" Erika said, feeling as proud of Charlotte as her daughters must.

The last time Erika had heard from her biological mother, Lena was traveling the country with a truck driver boyfriend. Her previous relationship, with a man she met over the Internet, had eventually fizzled. In a moment of tenderness a year or so ago, Erika sent Lena a photo of Aaron. When she never heard back, she realized little had changed. Her mama was still a rolling stone.

The more Erika frequented church and listened to Micah share wisdom from the Bible, the more she understood what Serena meant when Serena talked about God "sending" people or "using" people to touch others.

When Erika had needed it most, God had sent her what she'd always been missing. The love still wasn't coming from Lena, whom she thought was the only one that could give it. Instead, Charlotte, who had seen her through the lowest points in her life, had been tapped for the job, and Erika thanked God every day.

Charlotte's children had long ago accepted Erika as a surrogate sibling and were excited to see her and her friends.

"Mom was so happy that you were coming and that your friends were joining you," Geri said. "She talks a lot about you, Serena. It's nice to finally put your face with your name."

By the time all of the women had changed into semi-formal wear for the party, which was being held at a nearby church fellowship hall, Charlotte's two sons arrived in their SUVs to transport them. Gerald's and Raymond's wives had driven together with their children and were already waiting at the church.

The evening went quickly, and after Charlotte's boss, Audrey, gave her farewell speech, she called Charlotte to the podium.

Charlotte motioned for Erika and for her daughter, Tanya, to come forward.

Tanya and Erika exchanged curious glances but did as instructed. They stood just behind her and waited for more direction.

Charlotte thanked Audrey and her colleagues and shared her story of fleeing an abusive marriage. Then she gestured for Tanya and Erika to join her. Her daughter stood to her left and Erika to her right.

"I asked these ladies to come up here because they represent why I do what I do every day at Naomi's Nest and why I will continue to further the work of this shelter as executive director."

Erika was stunned to see tears fill her friend's eyes. In all the years they had known each other, she had only witnessed Charlotte's strength. But as Charlotte turned to her eldest daughter, Tanya, the tears flowed freely.

"The night I left my husband, with Tanya and her three

siblings in tow, this girl looked at me with her big brown eyes and asked, 'Mommy, do you know what you're doing? How do you know they won't beat you at the shelter?'"

Everyone joined Charlotte in laughing at the memory.

"I knew then that I had something on my hands. But more importantly, I knew it was time to go, to save my life and hers, so she wouldn't grow up thinking beatings and verbal abuse were signs of love. Every time I look at Tanya and Geri and my sons, Gerald and Raymond, and see what beautiful lives and families they now have, I know that coming to Naomi's Nest gave me the gift of a new start."

There wasn't a dry eye in the room by the time Charlotte turned toward Erika, who was dabbing her cheeks with a napkin.

"And this little bitty thing here—" Laughter filled the room as Charlotte leaned over and hugged Erika, who stood a foot shorter than she. "She came to the shelter afraid of everything—the spiritual music I played, the prayers and Scriptures that flowed freely from my lips, the unconditional friendship I offered. But when I figured out what Erika needed, I was able to reach her.

"That's all we have to do with anyone we know who's hurting. Figure out what they need, and when you fill that need, they'll open their hearts to you and to all the other good things you have to share with them."

She smiled at Erika.

"Erika's biological mother is still alive, but when I met her, she needed someone to scold her when she was wrong, hold her when she was scared, and cheer her on when she was on the right track. It has been a blessing to fill that role in her life and to be there for her son as well."

Charlotte faced the podium and the audience again.

"I share all that to say that what has brought me from battered wife to executive director is the same thing that will sustain each of us on our journeys—L-O-V-E. Under my leadership, love will continue to be integral to the mission of Naomi's Nest, along with securing grant funds, donations, and the volunteer support we desperately need. If you haven't already done so, consider joining us in this important and lifesaving work."

○

Hours later, back at Charlotte's apartment, the mood was still solemn. Kami flipped channels with the TV remote while Erika and Tawana played checkers.

"What gives, ladies?" Charlotte asked when she entered the condo's sitting area after changing back into her overalls. "It's only 9:30. I know you aren't tuckered out already. What do you want to do?"

Serena, who was sprawled on the floor, flipping through recent issues of *Essence*, looked up and smiled. "That speech rocked our world, Charlotte. We feel like we're in the presence of greatness. What are we supposed to do?"

Charlotte shook her head and took the remote from Kami. "Y'all are pitiful. Come down off the mountaintop and let's do something. I'm sixty-one years old and have more energy than you guys. I know you didn't travel from Richmond just to sit around like little old ladies. If nothing else, want to rent a movie?"

Erika, Serena, Tawana, and Kami looked at each other and answered in unison:

"*Set It Off.*"

28

Charlotte sat on the floor, Indian style, and watched her guests read the scrolling movie credits. Each seemed lost in her thoughts.

"What'd you think?" she asked when the screen finally faded to black.

Kami nodded. "Pretty good for a ten-year-old movie. I understand why the four of them were frustrated. Society had kicked them down, and this was the only way they knew how to kick back."

Charlotte turned to Tawana. "Which one of the characters did you identify with most?"

Tawana, who sat on the floor with her back against the sofa, chewed on her bottom lip before responding.

"I could have been Tisean, the character played by Kimberly Elise, for a number of reasons," she said softly. "I had a baby when I was really young, and I've made mistakes with guys like she obviously did."

Serena, who had stretched out on the love seat, pushed up on her elbow and looked at Tawana. Tawana's quiver-

157

ing voice told her this was more than just simple reflection over a movie.

Tawana continued. "But you know, I could also relate to Stony, Jada's character, because like her, sometimes I just want to run and hide from my past and from all the pain that lingers there."

Tawana pulled her knees up to her chest and burrowed her head into them.

Charlotte turned toward Serena. "What about you, Mrs. First Lady?"

Serena wanted to go over and comfort Tawana, but she respected Charlotte enough to trust how she was handling the situation. She sat up and furrowed her brow.

"Hmmm . . . I think I related to Queen Latifah's character and Vivica Fox's," she answered. "I was Cleo when I was in my twenties and very angry at my parents for some of their choices. But thank God, unlike her, I had an opportunity to learn and grow, and that anger transformed into a powerful life lesson."

Serena sighed. "I guess I relate to the want-to-be-perfect aspect of Vivica's character, Frankie, now. I have to be honest: Some days this stay-at-home mommy gig kicks my butt. The kids seem to run wild and wear me down, the house is never clean enough, my attention is divided between them and Micah, and . . ."

Her own urge to cry caught her off guard. "And I don't know how I'm going to do it again when this new little one comes. I think I might just lose it."

She hadn't meant to announce her pregnancy like this, but oh well.

Erika and Kami came over and hugged her.

"You know we're here for you, Serena; you don't have to be perfect," Erika said. "Remember that grace you're always talking to me about? Don't you think it's time you extended it to yourself?"

Charlotte seemed to be on a mission. She turned to Kami and smiled gently. "I'm really not trying to bring all of you to tears; I just want to know where your hearts and heads are."

She surveyed each of the women. "When you get a girlfriend weekend like this, use it wisely. Have a ball, let your hair down. But make it memorable for more than just the fun of it. That's what will really bind you together as sisters."

She looked at Kami again. "You're still young, but did anything in the movie speak to you, other than what you shared earlier?"

Kami shrugged and looked at Serena, Erika, and Tawana.

"I don't know that the movie touched me so much," she said. "It was entertaining, and I got the symbolism, but I guess hearing how it resonated with Tawana and with my sister means even more. They're the ones teaching me about real life, by just watching them handle it every day."

Charlotte nodded, then pointed at Erika. "You know I saved you for last."

Erika gave a half smile. "That's what I was afraid of."

She removed her arms from around Serena and folded her legs under her. She looked toward the ceiling to think about her answer.

"I saw a piece of myself in all of the characters, I guess," Erika said. "I understood Tisean's pain in not being able to care for her child; I've struggled with a difficult past like Stony and still struggle to forgive my mother for loving the men in her life more than me; I worked in corporate America, like Frankie, but lost my status there because Elliott forced me to stay home and cater to his needs; but most of all, I've felt anger similar to Cleo's because I was a battered wife. I guess I'm still angry at Elliott and the hold he has over me."

Charlotte leaned forward. "Ah, now we're getting somewhere."

Erika looked at her and frowned. "What does that mean?"

"You answer my questions first," Charlotte said. "What kind of hold does Elliott still have over you, after all these years?"

Erika hesitated. "Elliott wants a divorce so he can get remarried."

"And?"

"What do you mean, 'and'?" Erika was indignant. "He's spent the past two years telling me he wants to reconcile and that he's seeking professional help so we can put our family back together. He sends me cards in the mail every two weeks trying to romance me. Now out of the blue he says, 'Forget it, it's over'?"

Charlotte didn't respond.

"Hello?"

"I want you to hear yourself," she told Erika.

"What do you mean, Charlotte?" Erika asked. "I don't understand."

"Erika, listen to yourself. Ask yourself what you're so upset about."

The room fell silent while Erika processed Charlotte's instructions.

"Are you upset because you really love Elliott? Do you want to spend the rest of your life with him?" Charlotte asked the questions slowly.

"Or, are you ticked off that all this time you felt like you were getting revenge by stringing him along? He obviously wanted you back, but you were going to make him pay for the pain and suffering he caused you. You did it by watching him long for you. Now that he's trying to tell you goodbye—or at least pretend like he's going somewhere—your game plan is ruined."

Serena saw Erika's defenses crumble.

Charlotte didn't force an answer. Instead, she rose from the floor and looked at the grandfather clock in the corner.

"Almost midnight, ladies," she said and headed toward her room. "Feel free to stay up as late as you want. I'll see you in the morning. Good night."

Erika, Serena, Tawana, and Kami stared at Charlotte as she strolled to her room and closed the door behind her.

They sat in silence, until Tawana said what each of them was thinking.

"This has got to be a sick joke. She leads us into a Dr. Phil session and then goes to bed?"

No one laughed.

Erika looked at her bare ring finger, then at each of her friends.

"Now I know why she encouraged me to invite you guys," she said. "She wanted to bring all of us to our knees."

29

The smell of bacon, omelets, and coffee lured the sleeping beauties toward Charlotte's cozy kitchen.

Kami and Tawana had shared the sleeper sofa and were the first to rise when they heard Charlotte bustling at the stove. She refused their offers to help, so they made small talk, careful to avoid a return to the previous night's weighty conversation. Tawana had picked up the morning copy of the *Washington Post* and was intrigued to find a lengthy profile of Neal Lewis's family and details about his upcoming trial in Richmond.

Serena and Erika emerged from the guest bedroom just as Charlotte was setting plates of steaming food in front of each chair at the table. Before she took a seat, she placed a deep purple chamois bag next to each place setting.

"What is this, Charlotte?" Erika asked. "Don't tell me you went out and bought us gifts. You're the honoree this weekend, not us."

Charlotte responded by extending her hands. When the five of them were touching, she led a brief prayer to bless the food.

She raised her head and reached for the saltshaker. "I know I don't need it, but it won't hurt just this once."

"Don't you say that every time?" Erika asked. "Back to my question. Gifts?"

Charlotte took a bite of the omelet and motioned for the others to eat as well. She looked at Erika. "Let me do my thang, okay?"

Erika laughed at Charlotte's attempt to be hip. "Okay, *Miss* Thang."

Charlotte ate slowly, savoring each bite. Little was said as they enjoyed the meal.

"Now that you're all sufficiently curious, I guess I can explain the bags or, better yet, what's in them," Charlotte said and took a sip of her third cup of coffee.

"Finally," Erika said. She leaned forward and rested her slight weight on her elbows.

"When Erika told me you were coming up with her for the weekend, and knowing how close you all are, I thought this would be a great time to share the gift that a good friend shared with me soon after I moved into Naomi's Nest two decades ago with my children.

"Harriet Washington picked me up one Sunday and took me and the children to church," Charlotte said. She fixed her eyes on an abstract painting above her sofa, clearly traveling back in time.

"After service, her sisters agreed to watch and feed the kids while the two of us went out to eat. She took me to a restaurant on the outskirts of the District, where we could talk privately. She gave me a small bag similar to the one you're receiving."

Charlotte pulled a black pouch from her shirt pocket and

poured its contents into her palm: three loose pearls—one bronze, one translucent, and one turquoise.

She asked her four guests to open their bags. They each poured three pearls of varying colors into their palms.

"Like Harriet told me that day, and I now firmly believe, pearls symbolize life, and how God can create something beautiful out of tragedy, shame, or sin, as long as we're willing to be transformed.

"A brief science lesson, okay?" Charlotte continued when each of the attentive women nodded.

"Pearls are formed inside of oysters or other mollusks living in the sea. Unless something gets inside of an oyster's shell, the oyster just swims along in life with no need to change or grow or pay attention to the outside world."

Serena smiled.

Charlotte nodded. "I'm embellishing a little here, just so you can picture what I'm trying to convey, but this is grounded, for the most part, in fact.

"So, the oyster is just swimming along, until an irritant, a foreign object, somehow gets under its shell and begins to infiltrate its layers," she said. "An oyster's body reacts to the foreign object by producing a substance that forms hard and shiny layer upon layer around the irritating object, to isolate and surround it.

"In doing so, the oyster accomplishes two tasks: it protects its body and creates something lasting and beautiful—a pearl. Think about it, Erika, Serena, Tawana, and Kami. We aren't much different, are we?"

Erika lowered and shook her head. "Wow."

Charlotte continued.

"We are like those oysters in many ways," she said. "Irritants, or foreign objects, infiltrate our lives in the form of bad choices, jealousy, fear, deep loss, and countless other challenges I could name. We choose how to handle the things that come, either by rallying our strength and faith and finding a way to go on, or by giving in to the pressure and giving up.

"When we choose to stand up inside and protect our spirits, our hearts, and the essence of who we are, we produce a substance similar to what the oyster produces to form the layers of a pearl. In us, it's called character, integrity, grace, courage, and the ability to love ourselves and others, with no strings attached."

Charlotte looked at the four women and smiled.

"I was glad when you guys chose a movie last night about four women struggling to find their place in society, however wrong they were in going about it. God is something else. He knew I was planning to share this with you this morning and that your hearts had to be open to seeing yourself as you are, but also with a vision for what you are becoming."

Charlotte spread her arms wide again.

"The things we've been through, or are going through, are producing layers in us. We are becoming more than our circumstances. We're multicolored and multilayered."

Charlotte took Tawana's hand and gently squeezed it.

"I heard the regret and shame in your voice last night," she said. She pointed at one of her three pearls, which she had set on the table, on top of her black bag.

"See this?" she asked Tawana. "This is what you are

becoming. A precious, beautiful jewel. Of course, it's going to take some 'irritants' to get you there.

"I don't know all of your missteps and mistakes, but God does." Charlotte looked at Tawana first and then at each of the women at the table. "He sees those things that have hurt you or left you feeling less than good enough, and he's begun a good work in you anyway."

Tawana frowned and shook her head. "Some of the things I've done or have almost done are pretty terrible."

Charlotte shrugged.

"The very things you're condemning yourself for are issues that other people battle too, Tawana," she said. "The Bible isn't exaggerating when it essentially tells us that there's nothing new under the sun. The longer you live, you're going to face some things that you think will take you out."

She picked up her pearls again. "When those times come, remember these loose jewels and what they represent: they are fragile and need to be handled with care, but they also are resilient and they represent your struggles, your ability to survive, and your beauty.

"My pearls are bronze, pink, and white, for no particular reason other than Harriet wanted me to know that the situations that were shaping me at that time might have a different purpose for someone else facing the same issues. We come in all shapes, sizes, and colors, determined by the shape, size, and color of the irritants that float into our lives."

Serena looked at her cultured pearls, which were lavender, pink, and teal. Kami's were white, steel blue, and gold. Erika and Tawana also had unique colors.

"Around this table, I see in each of you the scars and the choices that have brought you to this place in life," Charlotte said. "You're all translucent yet very different, and you are supposed to be. You're the color of water that ebbs and flows with the tides of life. You're watercolored pearls."

30

Erika paused at the door, with duffel bag in hand, and hugged Charlotte goodbye.

"I still can't get over it," she said. "We came up to celebrate you, and you turned the tables on us. Thank you for my pearls. I love you, Charlotte."

The two women gripped each other and held on.

Serena cleared her throat. "I hate to interrupt, but can the rest of us get some love too?"

Charlotte and Erika laughed.

"I tell you, you grown women are so jealous!" Charlotte playfully spanked Serena's hand and pulled her toward her for a hug.

"I know it's hard with your mother gone," she whispered in Serena's ear. "You know I'm always here for you if you need me."

Serena nodded as tears welled up in her eyes. She had come to accept that she would never get over her mother's death; instead, she had learned to live with a broken heart.

Charlotte stood back and looked at her. "I know how

you're struggling with the kids and your new season in life, but you aren't alone. I might have sounded like I had it all together when I shared last night about raising my four children in the shelter, but believe me, Serena, there were days when I thought I was losing my mind, or that I was going to lose my children because I couldn't handle the pressure.

"God always sent angels my way when I was at my weariest. Always. He'll do the same for you, especially with the new baby coming."

Charlotte touched Serena's belly and smiled. "He didn't open your womb for nothing; he's walking this purpose and this path with you."

Serena hugged Charlotte again. "Thank you."

The return trip to Richmond was just as enjoyable, if less boisterous, than the ride to D.C. had been. The four friends marveled at how Charlotte managed to be so giving to everyone she met.

Kami held up her chamois bag. "I'll never forget what it means to be a watercolored pearl."

Serena, who was riding in the rear passenger seat this time, patted her sister's hand. "You're blessed to be finding out what that means at eighteen, Kami. Remember what Charlotte told us when things get difficult at Hampton or in your relationship with Kevin. I think it's wise of you two to be open to dating other people, especially since he's joining the Navy and you'll be meeting a slew of new folks. You've got years and years to add the layer of a long-term committed relationship. Right now, focus on getting to know yourself."

Kami winked at Serena.

"Gotcha, sis," she said.

In the front passenger seat, Tawana stared out of the window at the bland scenery of trees and brush they sped past. How had Charlotte known what she needed to hear?

I know all things.

Tawana smiled and looked toward the sky, where one cumulus cloud after another seemed to guide the car toward home.

Of course. God had orchestrated this. Her life finally seemed to be falling into place.

She had stopped drinking heavily before moving in with Micah and Serena because she didn't feel right bringing her stash of wine to their place.

It turned out, though, that she hadn't really needed it. Neal Lewis's murder trial was six weeks away, and she and the other lawyers had been working thirteen-hour days. When she was home, she spent what time she could with Misha before falling into bed.

Tawana realized she hadn't had to fend off loneliness, because she had landed in a cocoon of friendship at work and love in the McDaniels's home. The images of her numerous one-night-stand boyfriends didn't parade through her dreams as frequently as they once had, either.

One of those dates still haunted her, though. She cringed when she recalled how she had tried to sell her body to Grant and had wound up in his bed anyway, on his terms.

What was I thinking?

She'd been asking herself that question for weeks now and praying that Grant wouldn't tell their mutual friend Elizabeth what had transpired. She also had been praying for God to forgive and to help her forgive herself.

This morning, though, Charlotte's wisdom, kind words, and gift of pearls had helped free her from her demons of the past. She couldn't go back in time and alter the choices she had made, but if she concentrated on moving forward and on consciously becoming the person she longed to be, eventually the past wouldn't matter as much.

Tawana looked at Erika, who kept her eyes on the road while she drove and hummed along to songs on the India. Arie *Testimony* CD.

Erika was so beautiful, Tawana thought as she watched her. Couldn't she see that she didn't need Elliott to make her happy? Didn't she remember who the true source of that emotion was?

Tawana laughed silently at herself. *Look at me, trying to tell someone how to fix her life, when I'm always going in circles.*

That was the funny thing about people, Tawana was realizing; one could so easily see the gem in others while missing their own precious stone, or they mistakenly believed theirs shined brighter than everyone else's.

Help me get it right, Lord. I'm tired of trying on my own, she prayed.

When Erika sailed past the Doswell exit, which led to King's Dominion amusement park just north of Richmond, Tawana grabbed her purse to rummage for some gum. She felt her cell phone vibrating and hit Talk just before the call was routed to voicemail.

"Hey, Mama, we'll be at the house in about twenty minutes," Tawana said. "Why aren't you at church? Didn't want to take the brood of kids?"

Tawana's eyes grew large. She turned to Serena.

"Micah's trying to reach you. Stillwell Elementary is under water."

31

Serena reached into her purse and pulled her black flip phone from its case. She gasped. Micah had tried to call at least ten times.

She had turned the phone on vibrate at Charlotte's party and had never switched it back to the ring tone. Before she could dial Micah's number, the phone chimed.

"Micah? What happened?"

The silence on the other end made her heart flip-flop.

"You almost home?" he asked.

Micah sounded deflated. Serena wanted to ask a thousand questions.

"Yeah, babe," she said softly. She gripped the phone so tightly that her knuckles glistened.

"It's bad, love," he said. "I went in this morning to open the school as usual, and Mr. Bracey met me in the parking lot. It started raining Friday after you left, and didn't let up until this morning.

"Water filled the third grade wing up to the students' desks. It didn't stop there this time. The gym, the cafeteria, and the school office also flooded, at least two feet. Mr. Bracey is worried about mold."

Serena was speechless. Thank God the school term had ended on Friday. At least the kids wouldn't be affected.

"How did you let the congregation know we weren't having church today?"

"I stood in the parking lot with Mr. Bracey and asked everyone who came to stay so we could have a group prayer. The principal, Mrs. Weldon, showed up to check on the school office and wound up joining us.

"We gathered for a little over an hour. I told Ms. Carter to take the boys and Misha home, but I'm still here, trying to see how I can help clean up."

Serena knew what this meant. New Hope Community Ministries would no longer be meeting at Stillwell Elementary School. The question now was whether they'd have somewhere to meet at all.

She knew this was going to work out; God hadn't failed them yet. But she also knew how Micah must feel. He had been removed by force twice—first by the officials of Standing Rock Community Church and now by Mother Nature.

"I'll be there as soon as I can, babe," Serena said softly.

Erika looked at Serena in the rearview mirror as she barreled toward South Richmond.

"Tell him we'll all be there."

32

Tawana crawled into bed next to Misha, just before midnight. Events of the evening tumbled through her mind. She had spent hours at Stillwell Elementary, helping Micah, Serena, Erika, and dozens of New Hope members mop and clean the school's classrooms and hallways once the standing water had been pumped out of the building.

By nightfall, the soggy desks, books, and who knows what else had begun to fill the building with a stench.

"City and school officials probably won't let us back in here, after today," Micah had told the members who had gathered. "They have folks coming to clean up, but this was our church home. Let's show the school staff we support them and try to salvage whatever materials we can."

Mr. Bracey returned around eight o'clock to lock the doors. "It's getting dark, and we don't know if snakes or other critters are lurking in this water," he said. "Time to go. Thanks for your help."

In the parking lot, Tawana watched from a distance as Serena embraced a forlorn Micah and talked softly to him. She thought about the words of wisdom Charlotte had shared that morning and knew that even this experience was going to make them all stronger.

God, thank you for the blessing in this.

When she had finally arrived at the McDaniels's house, all was quiet. Ms. Carter had put the children to bed and was watching news reports about the flood and the fifteen South Richmond families that had been displaced. TV anchor Sabrina Shaw had interviewed Stillwell Elementary's principal about the damage to the school and Micah about what the loss of this temporary headquarters would mean for his blossoming ministry.

A weary Micah shrugged on camera. "I don't know yet, but God knows. We'll have some answers before the week is over about where the congregation will meet next week. The one thing I can promise is that we aren't going away. New Hope Community Ministries is as much a part of the Stillwell community as this school. We'll get through this."

Ms. Carter turned off the TV and looked at Tawana. "You must be tired. How was your weekend?"

Tawana was thankful that sometimes Mama knew when to shed her tough demeanor. She approached her mother and bent down for a hug.

"The weekend was awesome, Mama," she said. "I'll have to tell you about it. Coming home to the flood was a letdown, but as Micah just said, we'll get through it. I'll be back in the office working on the Lewis case bright and early tomorrow."

Tawana plopped down next to her mother and watched part of an old movie before both of them decided to call it a night. Ms. Carter turned off the TV and quickly disappeared while Tawana prepared herself a cup of tea to sip until she fell asleep.

Micah and Serena walked in through the side kitchen door just as the phone rang. Tawana was climbing the stairs when she heard Micah's puzzled response.

"I'm sorry, you have the wrong number. No problem." He hung up and shrugged. "He was calling for someone named Elise."

"That's not the first time," Serena said. "I've taken several calls from people looking for an Elise."

Tawana paused on the stairwell, out of their view. The phone rang again and Micah sighed. "Didn't I just tell him . . . ?"

Before he could complete the thought, Tawana dashed into the kitchen and picked up the receiver.

"Hello?" she said breathlessly. "Oh, hi, Arlen. No, I'm okay, just had to run to get to the phone."

While she listened to Arlen explain how he must have dialed the wrong number seconds earlier, Tawana saw the recognition of what had just transpired register in Serena's and Micah's eyes.

"Glad you got me," Tawana told him. She tried to dismiss the shame that filled her being. "What's going on?"

Serena and Micah had waved good night and gone up to their room. She knew she'd have to explain the "Elise" thing later, but for now, she was intrigued by Arlen's reason for calling.

Neal had been asking for her over the weekend. He wanted to talk to her about the mystery girl he had come to Richmond to visit just before Drew Thomas disappeared.

"Why me?" Tawana asked.

"I don't know," Arlen said, "but we're willing to do whatever it takes to pull together this case. You're part of the defense team, so it's perfectly fine for him to request you. If he doesn't mind and you don't have a problem with it, I'd like to sit in too."

Tawana was glad he had offered. "That would make me feel a lot better."

Arlen agreed to meet her at the law firm at 9:00 a.m. so they could ride to the city jail together.

Tawana had taken her tea up to bed but found that for once it didn't help her relax. Misha's steady breathing filled the silence as Tawana watched the digits on the bedside clock switch to 3:00 a.m. Arlen's call had left her too curious to sleep. She gathered her notes on the Lewis case and sat in the kitchen, rereading them.

Maybe the interview this morning would provide the missing piece of the puzzle, she surmised, because something just didn't fit about why Neal would come to Richmond, get involved with a kid outside of his circle, and wind up being accused of that teen's murder.

Tawana accepted that sleep had indeed eluded her and showered and dressed for work. By the time she arrived at the firm, however, she could barely keep her eyes open.

She entered the office with her personal key, locked the door behind her, and made a pot of coffee. She retrieved Neal's file and studied the notes from interviews with Neal's friends in D.C., regarding what he had told them about his visits to Richmond. Tawana didn't feel herself falling asleep, but when she heard the office phone ringing, she jolted awake.

Who could be calling this early, except one of the partners? Or Arlen? Or was she dreaming?

This wasn't imagined. Someone was calling collect, from the city jail. At 7:20 a.m.

When the operator said Neal Lewis's name, a chill ran through her.

How did he know someone would be here this early? Why does he want to talk to me?

"Yes, I'll accept the call," she finally said.

The operator patched the call through. Tawana reminded Neal that she would be taking notes from their conversation and that the phone line from the city jail could be recorded.

Armed with that information, Neal seemed less inclined to talk. "Are you still coming down here? Today?"

"Yes, Neal. Arlen and I will be there in a couple of hours, so we can talk face-to-face. Was there something urgent you wanted to discuss right now?"

He hesitated.

"I'm ready to tell the truth."

33

Tawana knew from her law school training that "the truth" didn't have to be the same as "the story" the team crafted for Neal's defense. The goal in this case, as in any other, was to produce enough reasonable doubt to yield a "not guilty" verdict.

Given that, Tawana wasn't sure why Neal was now so intent on baring his soul. Arlen advised her not to ask, at least not until after they had gotten the information they needed.

"Whatever he has to say will likely help with our strategy for the case. We'll sit tight and listen and go from there."

Neal shuffled into the interview room this morning looking very different from the clean-shaven, out-of-place young man she had met a couple of weeks earlier.

His hair had grown an inch or so, a thin goatee covered his pimpled chin, and his confidence seemed to have diminished.

"Are you holding up okay in here?" Arlen asked.

Neal shrugged. "What do you think?"

A measure of the respect for older adults and authority that Neal had possessed a few weeks ago was gone. Tawana recognized it instantly; she had regularly witnessed its erosion in the mindset of her childhood classmates and neighbors. Before she had even sought God, his grace had saved her from that fate.

"It's your job to get me off," Neal told Tawana and Arlen. "Let's get to it."

After reading the article in the *Washington Post* over the weekend, she understood his attitude. Along with dissecting his family's influence in D.C.'s social and financial circles, and emphasizing Neal's privileged upbringing, the article implied that Stanford University officials had withdrawn his academic scholarship and were contemplating revoking his offer of admission. Tawana wondered if he had read it.

Arlen pulled out a miniature tape recorder, and Tawana placed a notebook and pen on the table.

"You ready?" she asked.

"Ready," Neal said. "But no recorder."

Arlen returned the digital cassette player to his briefcase and grabbed a notepad and pen.

Neal didn't waste time. He fixed his eyes on Tawana and began.

"I think you know the girl I came to Richmond to visit."

Tawana's interest was piqued. Since she had grown up in the city, it could be anybody.

"Okay . . . ," she said expectantly.

"Victoria Miller."

Tawana gasped. Bethany and Ian's daughter? "How . . . ?"

Then she remembered what he had already shared about the girl: they had met at an exclusive party in D.C., which sounded fitting for Bethany, and as a by-product, Victoria, who was being groomed to emulate her mother.

Neal launched into his explanation. "She and one of my classmates, Milania Webb, met at a summer equestrian camp and hit it off. Victoria was something else. She walked into Milania's party as if she were the host."

Neal smiled at the memory. "Everything stopped. She was digging the attention and I was digging her.

"We wound up dancing and talking most of the night, which made my girlfriend mad, but I didn't care; I knew I could make up with her the next day.

"Before Victoria left for the night, we shared our plans for the fall and what we wanted to do after college. She's beautiful, but she also knows what she wants out of life. I like that about her."

Tawana nudged him along. "When did you first visit Richmond?"

"I came for the first time the weekend after we met. We kept it quiet, because like I said, I had a girlfriend —Lacey— and my parents liked her a lot," Neal said. "Victoria didn't want her parents to know, either, and specifically her father, because she said he was becoming really religious and was trying to get her interested in faith and more focused on achieving her goals. She said her mother would understand, but for some reason, it was easier this way.

"She took me to Bottoms Up, the pizza place in Shockoe Bottom, and to Brown's Island where we sat and watched the river. The next time I visited, about two weeks later, I took her to dinner."

"Were these always weekend trips?" Tawana asked.

"Yeah," Neal said. "I would come down on Saturday morning so we'd have the entire day together."

Neal inhaled and began wringing his hands.

"After my seventh or eighth trip down, I decided to surprise her. My best friend, Steele, agreed to drive me, and our friend, Jamison, rode along. My parents had taken away my car because my grades had dropped to Bs in three classes. It shouldn't have mattered—I had already been accepted to 'the almighty' Stanford."

Tawana raised an eyebrow but didn't interrupt him.

"We got to Victoria's house and saw a Honda parked in the circular driveway, but I didn't think anything of it since my parents allow our maid and our gardener to park in our primary entrance. Steele and Jamison dropped me off and said they'd be back after scoping out the girls at the mall.

"I couldn't ring the doorbell because her parents didn't know about us, so I went around the back of the property to the pool. I was going to call Victoria's cell and tell her to meet me there.

"Then I heard voices and laughter, and I wondered if Victoria was swimming with her girlfriends. When I peeked through the gate, I saw her with a guy." Neal's voice grew strained. "With Drew."

"Drew?" Tawana didn't mask her surprise.

"They were sitting by the pool talking softly, and Drew was massaging her shoulders."

"What did you do?" Tawana asked.

"I walked in and confronted them," he said defiantly. "I asked her why he was there. She had told me her parents didn't allow her to date."

Neal's eyes grew hard. "Dude told me he was her boyfriend and that I needed to back off. He asked Victoria what *I* was doing there."

"What did she say?" Tawana asked.

"She tried to play it off and say that we were just friends. Drew got in my face and told me to leave his girl alone.

"I stormed around to the front of the house and called Steele and Jamison to come get me; I couldn't believe I was being played."

Arlen interjected. "Did you and Drew fight?"

Neal shook his head. "Victoria asked him to leave so her parents wouldn't ground her forever for having two guys at the house," he said. "Drew was angry, but he finally left, in his little Honda."

Tawana heard Neal's disdain. She wanted to kick him.

Be cool, you're a professional.

"What happened next?"

"Victoria came after me and said she was sorry; she hadn't known how to tell me she had a boyfriend, but she was trying to break up with him anyway," Neal said. "She said her mother didn't like Drew because he didn't live in their neighborhood or socialize with their friends or go to her school. She met him at the country club her family belongs to; he worked there as a lifeguard."

Tawana recalled the contempt she had felt growing up, from people who thought they were better than she was because she was poor. She tried to control her growing anger; Neal was a client, and he was entitled to his opinions, no matter how narrow-minded.

"Go on," she said softly.

"She begged me to come to her pool party the next

weekend and promised to introduce me to her friends. I believed she was really sorry about the Drew situation, and I couldn't tell her no," Neal said.

Arlen moved Neal on with another question. "The last time we talked, you said you came down without your parents' permission. How did you get here this time?"

Neal nodded. "I had come off punishment for my grades, but I knew my parents weren't going to let me drive to a party in Richmond when they didn't know the parents or the guest of honor," he said. "I told them I'd be spending the weekend at Steele's and that we would probably drive to Richmond to visit his cousin who's our age. They didn't question me. Steele actually stayed in the District that Saturday, and I came to Richmond alone, in my car."

"What happened when you showed up at Victoria's?" Tawana asked.

"Victoria introduced me to most of her guests and told them we'd met through a mutual friend," he said. "They thought it was cool that I'd come from D.C. We were having a good time until Drew showed up and started tripping."

Neal stared at a faded spot on the table. "Her friends didn't know him, either, except as the lifeguard at the club. Some of them asked why he was there. Others pretended they didn't see him."

A bitter laugh escaped him, but he quickly turned serious again. "He approached me and tried to start an argument. He got loud and started shouting that Victoria was using me. Her mother appeared out of nowhere and escorted me, Drew, and Victoria into a utility room connected to the pool house. She basically told us that she knew her daughter was gorgeous, but we weren't going to get 'ghetto' at her party."

Neal looked from Tawana to Arlen. "I told her she must not know who my father is. When I mentioned his name, her demeanor changed. She told me I could stay if I wanted, but she told 'pool boy' he had to leave."

"You mean Drew?" Arlen asked.

"Yeah," Neal said. "'Pool boy Drew.'"

"And then?" Tawana asked.

"She took Victoria's hand and led her back to the party," Neal said. "I laughed at Drew and told him the best man had won the right to stay, so he needed to leave. I tried to walk past him, but he lunged at me."

Neal shook his head as he remembered. "Something came over me; I let him have it."

Tawana leaned across the table and looked into Neal's eyes. "What does that mean, Neal? What did you do?"

"I'm a champion wrestler for my school. Drew swung at me, and I pinned him to the floor."

He wrung his hands and lowered his head. "I kept him pinned there until he stopped squirming. I didn't mean to seriously hurt him. I just wanted him to leave me alone."

Neal looked up at Tawana and Arlen. "When I sat up, Drew wasn't moving. He just lay there. I'm trained in CPR, so I checked his pulse and tried to revive him."

Tears filled his eyes and he looked from Tawana to Arlen.

"It was too late. I killed him. I killed Drew Thomas that day."

34

Erika sat behind the wheel of her car and stared at the house that had once been her castle.

Little had changed about the massive brick home since her middle-of-the-night escape; even the draperies she had custom ordered for the windows appeared to be the same.

How does this feel?

She asked herself that probing question because she knew it would have been the first one issued by Charlotte if she were along for the ride.

A familiar anxiety surfaced and she quickly thrust the self-examination aside. Enough reflection—she was here to get this over with. Aaron had been invited for a play-date and dinner at a preschool friend's house. Before she picked him up, she was going to have a straightforward talk with his father.

The visit to Charlotte's house over the weekend hadn't made her decision any clearer, but it had led her to believe that clarity would come in having a heart-to-heart discussion with Elliott so she could decide whether investing the time in starting over was worth a try.

Do you love him?

Another Charlotte question. Truthfully, not in the way she once had. She was not head-over-heels smitten with this handsome law partner to the point that she'd surrender her will again to make him happy.

Yet, if loving and pleasing God meant she should build a comfortable and committed relationship with Elliott for the sake of honoring her vows and for their child, she was willing to make that sacrifice. Even if it cost her the man she did love.

Thinking about her dilemma brought tears to her eyes.

She had sat on her sofa last night, staring at the television but seeing nothing. The words and images moved across the TV screen, but her mind kept replaying its own movies with scenes lifted from her memory bank:

She and Elliott dating in college.

She and Elliott on the beach in Jamaica, reciting their wedding vows before unknown, but kind, islanders.

She and Elliott at a local carnival recently, with Aaron walking between them holding each of their hands.

Erika had fingered the items on her lap—her Bible and the bag of pearls Charlotte had given her. She cherished them both, but there was no question which held more weight. She had to follow God's Word.

If nothing else, the weekend at Charlotte's had confirmed something she had wrestled with admitting for the longest time: her feelings for Derrick ran deep.

Being in D.C. and not having an opportunity to see him, or at least talk to him, had been difficult. She knew if she hadn't come, Derrick would have attended Charlotte's celebration. She also had accepted that if she weren't a married wife and mother, regardless of how long she and Elliott had been estranged, she would have no qualms about forging a relationship with Derrick.

He was a good and thoughtful man. He had shown her that consistently in the nearly four years she had known him. He had given her a chance when she came to him with a smidgen of talent, but no interior design degree and no formal design training.

Most of his colleagues would have laughed her out of their showrooms. Derrick had held her hand most of the way. He had been the first man to hold Aaron after the boy's birth and had reassured Erika that she was doing the right thing when she gave temporary custody of the baby to Serena.

There was no denying it.

I love him, she had whispered, acknowledging for the first time the emotion she'd been trying to suppress.

She wasn't sure, though, if acknowledging her feelings gave her the right to act on them. No matter how many justifications she came up with, she struggled with the notion that in the Bible, the author of Deuteronomy described divorce as the last straw for men and women who couldn't reconcile their differences.

Abuse was a valid reason to end a marriage. But as she had come to know God, she knew he expected his children to love and keep loving no matter what. She knew God had given Elliott the same grace he was extending to her, and if Elliott had changed, the Bible indicated that he deserved a chance at having his family restored.

So here she sat, with the sun setting, watching the house she thought she'd never enter again, preparing to ring the doorbell and ask to come in for a visit.

Erika forced herself to release her grip on the steering wheel and pick up her purse. Just in case Elliott lost his cool and flipped out, she had her cell phone, and her mace, ready.

If you're concerned, why are you doing this?

Erika ignored the voice and opened the car door. Before her feet hit the pavement, she heard a yelp that sounded almost human.

There it was again. It *was* a person's voice, and it was coming from the direction of Elliott's side entry garage.

Erika froze. Was she having flashbacks, or was someone inside that house being beaten?

35

She might have been stupid once, but she wasn't crazy enough to walk into danger again.

Erika jumped behind the wheel of her car and locked the door. She slid her window halfway down to listen for more cries and convince herself she wasn't hallucinating.

Should I call the police?

Erika had barely formed the question when she saw a woman run down Elliott's driveway, clutching her face and sobbing. The woman fled past her, in bare feet, with her long black hair flying behind her.

Erika's heart stopped. The woman looked nothing like her, but she saw in that instant what her future would be if she moved back into that house with her son.

She clutched her chest when, seconds later, Elliott stalked out of the garage and stood in the driveway with his hands shoved deep into his pockets.

His eyes were flaming, but he was silent, and Erika knew why. He would beat a woman fiercely behind closed doors, but he wasn't going to risk his reputation in public.

This woman must have caught him off guard by running away—something she had never been brave enough to do, Erika mused.

Erika started her car and slowly pulled away from the curb.

Elliott heard the engine and looked in her direction. The rage that had filled his eyes was temporarily replaced by shock.

Erika paused long enough to make eye contact with him. She wanted her eyes to speak for her this time. He got the message and bowed his head.

Thank you, God. I'm free. Tears showered Erika's cheeks as she uttered the prayer.

She drove slowly so she could see where the bruised and terrified woman might have gone. Seconds later, Erika found her at the entrance of the subdivision, sitting on a small stone bench surrounded by flowers and shrubs.

The woman was bent over, hugging herself and weeping.

Erika was afraid to leave her car, knowing that Elliott was prone to get into his vehicle and come search for one or both of them. She pulled to the side of the road and lowered her window.

"Mara?"

The woman raised her tear-streaked face and bruised eyes to Erika's. "How did you know my name?"

"I'm Erika, Elliott's former wife." A boulder of worries lifted from her shoulders when she uttered those words. Erika felt physically lighter.

"Let me help you," she told Mara. "Get in the car; I'll take you wherever you want to go."

Mara walked slowly toward the Lexus and stood at Erika's window.

"How did you just happen to be here, in this neighborhood, when I needed help? And how do I know I can trust you?"

Erika wiped her own tear-stained face with the back of her hand and smiled.

"The best and simplest answer to those questions is 'God.'"

36

Christmas in July would have a whole new meaning for Micah and Serena after this week.

Forget summer sales or early preparations for the official December holiday. For the McDaniels family, it symbolized the love and caring the Richmond community had shown New Hope Community Ministries since word spread about the damaging flood at Stillwell Elementary.

Five local pastors called Monday morning and offered to let Micah use their churches on Saturdays or late Sunday afternoons to hold New Hope's services. Others invited Micah's congregation to join their members for worship service.

Most powerful, however, had been a personal visit from Rev. Randy Tolliver, the elderly pastor of Zion Memorial Church, located about five miles south of Stillwell Elementary in South Richmond. He tracked down Micah after viewing Sabrina Shaw's TV segment on the flood and hearing Micah's comments during the piece. Over pancakes at an IHOP not far from his church, Rev. Tolliver had made an unusual request.

"We want your congregation to take over our church and allow us to blend in with you."

The Caucasian, white-haired minister and the dark-skinned, brown-eyed Micah gave each other a once-over and laughed heartily. In that instant, Micah knew that whatever this man said, he had a heart for God's people. That was enough to cement a friendship.

"Well, maybe 'blend' is not the word I'm looking for," Rev. Tolliver followed up. "How about 'merge' with New Hope members?"

"Why do you want to do this?" Micah asked.

"I'm seventy years old and I represent the average age of our sixty-member congregation, Rev. McDaniels," he said. "We haven't had new members in years, and we have this beautiful forty-thousand-square-foot church that includes a 600-seat sanctuary, a gym, and a two-story education building that needs to be filled with the light and love of Christ.

"I've seen and heard good things about your ministry for several years now. When I saw you on TV after the flood, God laid it on my heart to call you," Rev. Tolliver said.

"The deacons and trustees of the church—all five of them—have prayed about this, too. Zion is located in a neighborhood that years ago changed demographics, more fitting with the population you serve."

Rev. Tolliver didn't sugarcoat reality. "I'll be honest with you. We were the victims of white flight. Those of us who are still well enough to come on Sundays drive in from the suburbs or a nearby retirement home," he said. "But we have no clue about how to serve the growing African American and Hispanic population that surrounds the church.

"If you have a heart for God and for God's work in the mission field, you have to allow him to do new things in you and through you. This would certainly be a new thing for the silver hairs at Zion, Rev. McDaniels; but if God is giving us this opportunity to open his house of worship to others in the body of Christ, we want to accept it."

Micah was speechless.

Rev. Tolliver understood. "The magnitude of God's awesomeness can do that to us, can't it?"

They left the restaurant with the agreement that for the next six months, New Hope's thousand-plus members would worship and fellowship at Zion Memorial and use all of its facilities as desired. Micah offered to start a specific seniors ministry that could incorporate the needs of Zion's members, on Sundays and throughout the week.

If the trial period was a success, the two ministers agreed to evaluate from there how to move forward.

Micah walked Rev. Tolliver to his car and shook his hand. When the older minister drove away, Micah sat in his Jeep, in silence.

Lord, you never cease to amaze me, he prayed.

His heavenly Father's reply made him smile. *Don't ever think I will.*

Micah picked up the phone to call his wife.

37

What did you do with information that could send a person to prison? For the rest of his life? A person with morals would run straight to the police and do her civic duty. Unless, of course, you were a lawyer, bound by attorney-client privilege.

That's what dear little Neal was counting on, but as far as Tawana was concerned, he was a murderer who had lost his mind, and she wasn't going to contribute to the effort to set him free.

Tawana had been fuming all morning since she and Arlen had listened to Neal's confession.

"Why do you think he told us? And me, in particular?" Tawana asked Arlen again, as they ate lunch at a Subway restaurant near the firm.

Arlen, who had been just as shocked as Tawana, bit into his sandwich and shook his head. "I don't know, Elise. I'm still trying to figure this one out."

That was the other thing bothering her: How had Neal made the connection between her and Victoria since she was using the name Elise at the firm, instead of Tawana?

Micah and Serena might have figured it out after that Sunday night call from Arlen, but how would anyone else have known?

Tawana frowned and whispered across the table to Arlen, "How will knowing this information help us defend him if he's pleading 'not guilty'? Are we supposed to say the crime was self-defense? Or should we convince him to plead to a lesser charge, suited to an accidental death? I don't know if I can stay on this case, Arlen. I can't represent a confessed killer."

Arlen, who had paused between bites of his sandwich, gestured for Tawana to give him her hands.

Puzzled, she complied. He looked at her and smiled.

"Elise, take a deep breath."

He held her hands while she did so. "Take another one. Now, think about something higher and greater than yourself and ask for guidance. For me, it's God. I've already prayed for him to show me, and the entire firm, what we're supposed to do with Neal's confession.

"On the surface, it looks like we've got a guilty client with little remorse, who wants us to help him work the system. But looks can be deceiving. So calm down, let your mind slow down, and try not to fret. The trial is another three weeks away; we can take the rest of today and let this information gel."

Tawana cocked her head to the side and frowned at Arlen.

"What?" he asked, before taking another bite of sandwich.

"Who are you, and where did my colleague go? You know, Arlen Edwards? Attorney extraordinaire?"

Arlen laughed and wiped his mouth with his napkin. He wagged a finger at Tawana and finished chewing.

"Looks like you're learning more than one lesson today," he said. "First, never be shocked by anything a client confides in you. People who look 'newborn-baby innocent' could be Jack the Ripper. In the criminal defense world, you learn to consider everything and expect anything.

"Second, never let a man's bow tie and professionalism at work lead you to believe he's one-dimensional," Arlen said. "Those are two of my characteristics, but there's a lot more to me than you can see at first glance."

Tawana nodded.

Arlen Edwards wasn't hard on the eyes. His broad smile was the first thing she noticed about him. It lit up his full, caramel face. He kept his mustache neatly trimmed and always sported one of those bow ties he preferred with his custom shirts. Tawana had found him to be meticulous about his appearance and about his work, but not stuffy.

What had been most surprising was his apparent shyness. She questioned him about it one night over a late working dinner, and he downplayed it.

"I'm not bashful when it comes to things or people I care about," he had responded. "That includes the people I'm helping receive a fair day in court."

Tawana had learned that he was a fellow U.Va. alum who had graduated six years before she earned her undergrad degree. Arlen had attended law school at the University of Richmond. However, today was the first time he had mentioned his faith.

"I know there's more to you than meets the eye, Arlen," she said as she polished off her sandwich. "But do you have to peel back the layers so slowly? Every day it's something new."

He slid out of the booth to dump his tray and refill his soda.

"That's the point, Elise."

38

Erika didn't know much about Elliott's fiancée, but one thing was immediately apparent: Mara was smart.

When Erika had offered to help her leave Elliott's subdivision, Mara accepted the ride only after reviewing Erika's driver's license.

"Now you know where I live, my height, weight, and age," Erika commented as she pulled away from the curb. "Where do you want me to take you? Home? To the hospital?"

Mara pointed to her eyes, both of which were bruised and rimmed with black. "How about the police station? Elliott has lost his mind."

Erika paused at the stop sign and stared at her passenger. "You're pressing charges?"

Mara returned the stare. "Wouldn't you?"

"I should have."

Mara sat back and fell silent. Erika turned onto Beach Road so she could head toward Route 10 and the county police department headquarters.

"He beat you," Mara said softly. "That's why you left him."

Erika glanced at her. "You didn't know?"

"How would I? I moved here from California eighteen months ago. I'm a legal secretary and met Elliott at a conference a little over a year ago," she said. "The story I got was that you were having an early midlife crisis and that soon after your son's birth, you decided you wanted to be free."

Erika laughed bitterly. "He told you that? And to think I almost took him back."

Mara shook her head. "I knew that was what he was up to. That's how I got these black eyes. I was cleaning out his car and stumbled across a card addressed to you. I opened it and read his note about loving you still and asking you to let him know your decision. How could he be writing that and telling me he wanted to elope soon?"

Mara ran her fingers through her hair with one hand and massaged her bruised cheek with the other. "At first he tried to play it off and say it was an old card, something he had purchased before we started dating. But I've been in that Mercedes a gazillion times; if that card had been there all that time, believe me, I would have seen it before today."

Erika wanted to laugh out loud and do a jig. In Mara, Elliott had met his match. She listened and tried to keep a straight face.

"Then, when he realized I wasn't going to fall for the okey-doke, he changed his story and said sending you the card was part of his plan," she said.

"He said he was stringing you along to keep you happy until you agreed to give him joint custody of his son. After we got married, then he would petition the court to give him full custody."

Erika almost broke her neck. "What?!"

Mara waved her off. "Don't even worry yourself, Erika. If he had sought custody, who do you think would have cared for the child? Not him. Do I look like I want some baby mama drama?

"I told him he had lost his mind. That's when he lost his temper and went off on me."

Mara turned and faced Erika. "I'm thankful for your help, but how did you just happen to be in the neighborhood?"

Erika started to give her a simplistic answer but thought better of it. "Mara, I've been wrestling for a long time with whether to end my marriage to Elliott, even though we haven't lived together since the night Aaron was conceived."

Mara frowned.

"I left Elliott on the night of our fourth wedding anniversary and lived in a shelter for battered women for over a year. That's where I was living, in hiding, when Aaron was born.

"I returned to Richmond only when I felt reasonably sure that Elliott wouldn't try to kill me," Erika said. "I was just that afraid of him. I wasn't wise enough to do what you're doing now, and put an end to the abuse when it started.

"Don't go back to him, Mara. I'm not going to, either."

39

Serena stood in the empty sanctuary of Zion Memorial Church and twirled around with her head thrown back.

She felt like breaking into song, but her heart was so full she didn't know which hymn or gospel tune would be most fitting to show her reverence for God.

Daddy, you have shut my mouth.

Indeed, she had been speechless two weeks ago when Micah had come home with the incredible news about New Hope Community Ministries' new home. God had a way of pulling off miracles in ways that defied reason.

She paused and hugged herself, including the baby growing inside of her that now protruded underneath her flowing dress. On mornings like this, when she was alone in God's presence, she didn't worry about what the future held. If God could bring Micah's ministry to this, surely he would help her in hers with her children.

Serena scanned the choir loft, which was raised on both sides behind the pulpit. She couldn't wait to stand there with New Hope's choir and belt out a song of praise.

This morning though, New Hope's and Zion Memorial's members were gathering for a one-hour ceremony to consecrate their union and their friendship before God. She thought about how the process would symbolize a marriage, and in her mind that was perfectly fine, because they were already brothers and sisters in Christ.

Erika walked in just as Serena sat in the front pew, and hugged her neck from behind. Serena looked up at her friend and squeezed her arm.

"Hey, you," she said. "Where's Aaron?"

"Outside with the nursery director. She's rounding up her supplies with help from the youths. This place is absolutely beautiful, Serena."

Serena nodded. "It is. New Hope's oysters and pearls."

They smiled at each other as Erika sat down next to her. "I'm on my way to transformation too."

Serena turned her body toward Erika's. "Anything new with Elliott?"

Erika nodded. "He goes to trial in a few weeks on assault and battery charges for injuring Mara, and the divorce proceedings are under way. I'm feeling pretty good."

Serena smiled. "You should."

Micah appeared in the pulpit and conducted a sound check on the microphone at the lectern before testing one at the front of the sanctuary near the altar. Members would use that one this morning if they wanted to come forward and share their thoughts about the merging of the two church congregations.

He waved to Serena and Erika from where he stood.

"*Good morning, ladies,*" he bellowed, doing a crackerjack James Earl Jones impersonation.

"Erika, what do you think of New Hope's new digs?"

She gave him a thumbs-up. "You must be doing something right, Pastor. God has blessed."

Micah pointed to Serena's growing belly. "In more ways than one."

Erika leaned over to rub Serena's stomach. "I know you probably hate when people do that, but I'm your sister."

"I guess you get special privileges, but don't do it in front of other people; they'll think that gives them the right to touch me too."

Micah approached them and sat on the pew behind them.

"What's the latest?" he asked.

Serena punched his arm playfully. "You're a day late and a dollar short, babe. We've already covered that."

Micah looked at Erika apologetically.

"I'm sorry," he said. "You know you're going to have to repeat yourself, right?"

The three of them laughed.

"Girl, where did you find this man?" Erika asked Serena. "Actually, Micah, I wish I had talked to you a long time ago, as my spiritual leader."

Serena sat up. "Should I leave you two to talk alone?"

Erika shook her head. "Please. You know everything he's going to hear anyway, Serena."

Erika turned toward Micah.

"Like I said, I know where I'm heading now, and I'm sure it's what God wants me to do. But I struggled for months, many months, over my marriage. I wanted to please God and obey what the Scriptures say about honoring marriage, and yet I never felt at peace about taking Elliott back. Now I know why, but how could I have known sooner?"

"You know, Erika," Micah began, "if I could interpret the Bible and provide a cut-and-dried answer for every situation that presents itself, I would be revered around the world. In other words, that would make *me* God.

"All of us, even ministers, struggle to understand and live by the Word of God, which can sometimes seem contradictory. You may read one proverb that declares a lazy man is headed for ruin and another passage, just a few pages away, that insists man must take adequate rest, because all striving is in vain.

"Regarding divorce, yes, the Bible clearly states that God despises broken vows," Micah said. "But it goes on to describe how divorces should legally be handled when they occur, because inevitably, humans do fail.

"I think what concerned you more than being outside of the law of the Bible, Erika, was being outside of God's favor."

Erika consumed Micah's insight. "Exactly," she said. "That was my issue."

"But if you look at the biblical passages on love and on a godly marriage, could you honestly say that was what you and Elliott had, or even had the potential of having? We know he physically abused you the first time around. After hearing how he pressured you with divorce papers and flaunted a fiancée in your face, not to mention the greeting cards he routinely sent, it sounds as if you were still being beat up—emotionally this time, and with the Scripture, because he dangled his newfound faith in your face to guilt you into taking him back."

Serena watched her friend's face. She could see validation settling in Erika's eyes.

Micah picked up a New Living Translation Bible from the pew rack in front of him. He turned to Romans, chapter 8, and read aloud:

> So now there is no condemnation for those who belong to Christ Jesus. For the power of the life-giving Spirit has freed you through Christ Jesus from the power of sin that leads to death. The law of Moses could not save us, because of our sinful nature. But God put into effect a different plan to save us. He sent his own Son in a human body like ours, except that ours are sinful. God destroyed sin's control over us by giving his Son as a sacrifice for our sins.

Micah closed the Bible and looked at Erika. "So essentially, we are supposed to honor God by being obedient to his laws. But our faith in Jesus covers us when we fall short. All that fretting and worrying you were doing, it wasn't in vain, because it showed God that you have a heart to live out his will.

"When you're facing a serious dilemma in the future, though, don't be afraid to seek help from a good Christian counselor," Micah said. "And ask God to keep you from getting caught up in dotting every *i* and crossing every *t*, to the point that you forget about his grace and mercy. He offers a new dose each day, enough for you and for me."

Erika smiled. "Thank you, Micah. I should have talked to you about this a long time ago. But you're right: I can learn and grow, even from this experience."

Micah rose from the seat and hugged Erika. He stooped to kiss Serena and rub her stomach.

"You gon' be alright, girl," he told Erika. "Now let me go get ready. We are about to have some *church* up in here!"

40

Today Tawana was meeting with him alone.

Arlen had to file a brief before the courts closed, and Brandon and Heather were busy on other aspects of Neal's case. Neal had asked to meet only with Tawana, and the partners had advised her to go.

"Given the bombshell he's already dropped in our laps, go prepared for anything," Bob Wallace said. "Call me the minute you leave and let me know what he says."

Tawana, who was still trying to figure out how she could withdraw from this case and save her law career, sat in the jailhouse meeting room twisting her pen around and around, attempting to quell the jitters.

Use your street smarts with this boy.

That unbidden advice surprised her. *I will, Lord, I will. Thank you.*

It amazed her how, in the short time she had lived with Serena and Micah, her coping mechanism had improved.

Wine was no longer her sedative, and manipulative men had lost their allure. Attractive guys still caught her eye, but she had decided at some point during the summer to seek God's heart, instead of a man's, until she had grown beyond her pattern of bad choices.

Brandon had cornered her in the law firm's boardroom one morning when they were alone and had caressed her with his hazel eyes. He was model gorgeous, with thick dreadlocks and pecs to die for, but when he offered a kiss, Tawana declined.

"You want to smooch before you ask for a date?"

A few months earlier she would have been charmed by his interest. Now she was able to accept the reality before her—Brandon's actions simply showed what he was really after. Heather had later confided that she hadn't been as savvy. She and Brandon no longer rode to work together or communicated outside the office.

When Tawana thought about the kind of person she wanted to date in the future, Arlen came to mind. He had not once flirted with her or indicated an interest other than professional, but she realized that he was a standard of what to look for: a man who loved God, was sure of himself, and had integrity in his work and private life.

That last thought caused her to cringe. In being Elise in one setting and Tawana everywhere else, what was she doing? Did her actions reveal character or the lack of it?

Before she could ruminate any longer, Neal entered the room and sat across from her. He gave her a calculated smile. "You're alone today."

Tawana assumed a streetwise persona and smirked. "What's this about, Neal? What do you want this time, to confess to another crime?"

"What if I did? You couldn't do anything about it. You're my lawyer."

She decided to call his bluff. "Technically, I'm not. I'm still in law school, in case you didn't know. I'm a summer associate at Wallace, Jones and Johns."

Neal grew pale.

Tawana leaned forward. "What? Are you worried now? Well, I'm here. Go ahead and spill the beans."

She prayed that the vein in her temple that pulsed when her heart was racing wouldn't give her away.

"What about the things I told you the other day when Mr. Edwards was here too?"

Tawana sighed and dropped the façade. "Look, Neal, I don't want to play games with you. Don't worry about any of us with the law firm breaking your confidences, as long as we're representing you. But I need you to stop being coy with me.

"Why did you confess the other day, and why specifically to me? What will you gain by announcing that you killed Drew Thomas?"

Neal lowered his head to the table and broke into sobs.

Tawana was startled. She sat back and waited for him to regain his composure.

"What is it?" she asked when he finally lifted his eyes.

"What do you do when you're just so tired of running and hiding and playing by everyone else's rules because you have none of your own?"

Neal's red eyes pleaded with her to provide an answer.

Tawana's heart softened. She had resented him the last time they met because he had so callously talked about people with less material wealth than his family possessed.

But today, he sat here in a jail cell, stripped of everything outside of himself. Without the car, the clothes, the status, and the money, he clearly was lost.

Tawana leaned toward him and spoke softly. "I'm only five years older than you, Neal, and I still have a lot to learn too. I'm still making mistakes and taking wrong turns as I figure out life. The only sure thing I can tell you is that for me, faith has been there through thick and thin."

She thought he would turn away, but Neal continued to listen.

"Until you look inside and figure out who you are and who you want to be, you'll always be floating from one thing to another, searching for validation. Those things or people could be good or bad for you, depending on the way their winds blow. Believe me, I speak from experience. It's important for Neal to be able to live with Neal, at the end of the day."

Now if I could just remember that for myself, Tawana thought.

"You're saying all the right stuff, but why do you call yourself 'Elise' when you're here and you go by 'Tawana' everywhere else?" he asked.

Tawana was busted.

"Like I said, I'm still a work in progress too, Neal," she said. "I've spent the last few weeks asking myself what I'm ashamed of, what I'm trying to hide by doing that. I don't have an answer yet. I'm curious, though. How did you know?"

Neal zeroed in on his hands, which he had connected in a teepee.

"It's a long story, but part of the reason I wanted you to come back today. I could tell that I shocked you the other day with my revelation, and I wanted you to know that I'm not this cold and calculating killer."

"But you confessed, Neal," Tawana said, shifting the conversation back to him. "And I'm not even sure if it was true self-defense, or if you pinned Drew in a wrestling move before he could attack you. My question is, how did you get his body out of there without being seen by somebody? You're from D.C. How did you find a place to dump Drew's body, and how did you turn up as a suspect?"

"Now you're asking the right questions," Neal said. "But if I answer them, both of us could be in jeopardy."

"Us?" Tawana asked.

"How much time do we have?"

41

Erika stood in front of the black double doors and prayed silently for the right words.

When she lifted her head, she almost jumped out of her skin. He had opened one door and was leaning against it, watching her.

"You going to stand there 'til kingdom come and not ring the bell?" He hadn't said it harshly, but he wasn't smiling. "What are you doing? Praying?"

Erika slowly put her two forefingers to her lips and kissed them. She pressed them to Derrick's lips, both to silence his questions and share her heart.

Derrick stared at her without responding. He took her hand and led her inside. They stood in his foyer, on this Sunday morning, silently sizing each other up.

She should have been in Richmond, at the fourth joint service for New Hope and Zion Memorial, but she had awakened with Derrick on her mind. She remembered how brusquely he had ended their last phone conversation and decided she didn't want a repeat episode. Plus, she just wanted to see him. She needed to see him.

Serena had agreed to keep Aaron for the day.

"If you love him, you need to let him know," she had advised. "It may be too late, but maybe not. You won't know if you don't try."

The two-hour drive to his home in Bethesda, Maryland, just outside of D.C., had given her time to think about what she would say, or should say, once she reached him.

Erika had arrived just before he would be leaving for Sunday morning service. She wore a silk summer dress and high-heeled sandals; maybe, if he were willing, she could join him.

Now here she stood, in his home, gazing into his beautiful eyes. Everything she wanted to say rushed through her mind. Her heart pounded.

He had let her inside, but what if he still told her goodbye? Erika knew she had no right to be here. She had strung him along and given him valid reasons to move on with his life, and the Bible they both revered had been her weapon.

Should she tell him that she loved him, she wanted to spend the rest of her life with him, she needed him, or . . .

Before she could say anything, she heard the *click-clack* of heels on Derrick's marble floors.

A thin, light brown woman with freckles and a short, layered hairdo rounded the corner. She put a manicured hand on one hip and paused to stare at Erika.

"Oh," she said and looked at Derrick. "Who is this?"

Erika thought she would die. Derrick moved to introduce her, but she waved him off. She didn't want him to see the tears or the searing pain emblazoned across her face.

She pulled the envelope she had brought for him from

her purse, laid it on a side table, and fled. It didn't matter now, but she wanted him to know that her divorce was final. She had made her decision.

Back in the car, she somehow put the key in the ignition and drove out of the neighborhood's unlocked gates. She couldn't call Serena, because she was in church. So was Charlotte. Who could she talk to now that she knew she had taken too long, wasted too much time, and finally lost the one man who had loved her? How could she continue to work for him?

Come to me and I will give you rest.

God hadn't failed her yet, but what could he do with the shattered pieces of her heart?

Erika pulled off an exit and into a gas station parking lot where she sat until she regained her composure.

She thought about how Derrick must have felt all those times she had pushed him away or asked him to wait. Life had a way of coming full circle; if he had endured the pain she was feeling right now, she couldn't blame him for moving on with his life.

The question now was, could she?

42

Serena was proud of herself.

Four months pregnant and no meltdown. She had been extra patient with the boys, willing to cut herself some slack on her lacking Martha Stewart and B. Smith abilities, and had even considered taking on some small freelance consulting work to keep her hand in the business world and bring in some extra income.

Having Misha around had been a joy. Serena had never spent this much time with her goddaughter. Misha was like a big sister to Jacob and Jaden, helping supervise their indoor playtime and read them stories, along with making them play along with her imaginary school or tea parties. Seeing her rough-and-tumble sons try to practice tea etiquette had been one for the scrapbooks.

Today, though, Kami had come by at just the right time.

One of the boys had poured his cereal on his brother, Misha was cranky from staying up late the night before to wait for Tawana to return home, and the washing machine had gone kaput. Kami showed up on her way home from the dentist and offered to help. Serena had literally shoved her dish towel into her younger sister's hands.

"Don't worry about the dishes in the sink—just watch the kids," she said, praying that Kami wouldn't protest. "I need some fresh air. Right now."

She was circling the block at a leisurely pace for the second time when she spotted Mrs. Brown, the retired teacher who lived a mile away and had babysat Aaron for her during his infancy.

Serena waved and crossed the street to say hello. Mrs. Brown was pulling two toddlers in a red wagon. She gave Serena a hug.

"You look beautiful!" said the stately woman. "And I see you have a little bun in the oven. When are you due?"

Serena rubbed her stomach. "December, and I have two boys already—twins."

Mrs. Brown's eyes widened. "Oh my goodness, no! How old are they? Do you still have my sweet little Aaron, too? How old is he now?"

The little girls climbed out of the wagon and knelt beside Mrs. Brown to pluck flowerlike weeds from the cracks in the sidewalk.

The difference in genders, Serena thought. *My boys would have crushed and smushed those weeds instead.*

"Jacob and Jaden are two; they'll be three in December," Serena answered. "Aaron is doing great. He turned four in April and is as smart as a whip, thanks in part to you."

Mrs. Brown clapped her hands. "That is such wonderful news. And he's back with his mother?"

Serena nodded.

"Erika lives here with him now. All is well."

"We live only a mile apart; it's surprising that I haven't seen you out walking before," Mrs. Brown said. "I watch these little cousins here now, and I usually take them out on nice days, in the mornings before it gets too steamy."

Serena looked sheepish.

"I'm only taking this walk to have some quiet time. I really should get out more with the boys. It's just that with the housework, keeping them busy, keeping on top of everything else . . . ."

Her voice trailed off and Mrs. Brown nodded. "Like your sanity?"

Serena smiled in embarrassment.

"I fully understand, Serena. These days, you moms try to do it all, but it's okay to have some help every now and then. You know what, why don't you bring the boys over one day a week so they can spend some time with me and give you a few hours to yourself, just to do nothing but relax or pamper Serena?"

Serena was taken aback. "How thoughtful of you to offer. I guess I hadn't thought about needing a sitter when I'm home all day. I'll check with Micah and see if it's in our budget."

Mrs. Brown smiled. "Check with him if you'd like, but this is my gift to you. There's no charge. Bring the boys over one day a week, the same day each week, for up to six hours.

"With a new baby on the way, and them so young, you've got to take care of yourself."

Serena protested. "Mrs. Brown, you can't work for free!"

She grasped Serena by the shoulders. "Let me handle

my business, okay? When I was a young mother, people opened their hearts to me. I'm just sharing my gift of caring for children with you. When you're older and have more time, you pass it on in your own unique way.

"Do you remember where I live?"

Serena nodded. "Your phone number too."

"Call me. I can't wait to meet the twins. Tell the rest of the crew I said hello."

When Mrs. Brown rounded the corner and was out of view, Serena looked heavenward.

Thank you for the angel visit today, she told God. *I needed that.*

43

Micah still hadn't gotten used to the idea of having an office where he could meet with ministry leaders, hold counseling sessions with members, and conduct other business.

Now that New Hope had space, he also had room for an assistant. Mrs. Billingsley, a retired executive secretary, eagerly accepted the part-time position.

After service today, she had tugged on his robe and whispered in his ear. "Great sermon, Pastor. A gentleman who attended the service this morning says he needs to talk with you. He says you'll know him—Deacon Ames?"

Micah nodded and scanned the mingling congregation to see if he could spot him.

"From Standing Rock Community Church," he said. "Ask him to meet me in the office in fifteen minutes."

Micah sat here now, waiting and wondering what had prompted this visit. He was somewhat angry that it was occurring now, weeks after he and his members had been in desperate need of support from area churches.

Micah had been grateful for the outpouring of love New

Hope had received from congregations throughout metro Richmond, but he had noticed Standing Rock's silence.

He stood to greet Deacon Ames when he heard the light tap on the door.

"Come in," he said.

Deacon Ames shuffled in with his cane, looking the same as he had when Micah left Standing Rock Community Church several years ago.

"Rev. McDaniels! How are you? Thank you for taking time to see me this afternoon."

Deacon Ames extended his hand to shake Micah's. Micah motioned for him to take a seat across from his desk.

"This is a surprise. What brought you over to South Side today? Standing Rock didn't have service?"

Forgive me for that dig, Lord.

Deacon Ames smiled self-consciously. "No, no, Standing Rock is still on the move," he said. "Rev. Lyons is expanding our TV ministry overseas and is getting more and more famous."

He suddenly turned the conversation to Micah. "I've been hearing great things about New Hope and the ministry work you're doing over here, and I thought I'd come for a visit. I hope . . . you don't mind?"

Micah felt bad. "Overlook me, Deacon. I didn't mean anything by that comment. You know you're always welcome in the Lord's house. I'm just the shepherd here; the doors are open to anyone."

Deacon Ames remained silent, but nodded.

"In fact," Micah said, "I think I've seen other Standing Rock members visiting in recent weeks. None has come over to say hello, but I've seen some familiar faces. It's a blessing that God isn't confined to one sanctuary, one style of worship, or one type of ministry. He's like the pearls my wife is always talking about—multicolored, multilayered, and offering something for everyone, in just the way their needs should be met."

Deacon Ames looked at Micah and smiled. "You're a good man, Rev. McDaniels."

Micah raised an eyebrow. "Where did that come from?"

Deacon Ames leaned forward on his cane and kept talking. "I wanted to meet with you today, after sitting in the service and being blessed by your sermon, and apologize for the way I treated you when you left Standing Rock."

Did Deacon Ames just apologize to me? This must be the day after never.

Micah wanted to ask him to repeat himself. Instead, he came around the desk and Deacon Ames hugged him. Micah towered over the elderly man; his head reached just above Micah's chest.

As they embraced, the deacon began to weep.

Startled, Micah pulled away. He helped Deacon Ames settle back into his chair and took the seat next to him.

"Is everything okay, Deacon? Do you need me to pray with you?"

Deacon Ames pulled a handkerchief from his pocket and mopped his face. He looked down at his hands, obviously embarrassed by his outburst.

Micah sensed that the deacon didn't want to say too much. He waited.

When Deacon Ames raised his head, he looked at Micah

and exhaled. "Sorry about that, Reverend. You know, if you'd be willing to pray with me, I would appreciate it. I found out last month that I have colon cancer."

Micah sat forward and touched Deacon Ames's shoulder.

The older man tried to smile. "Only a few people know, and Rev. Jason Lyons isn't one of them. I've left him message after message to call me, but he's too busy being fitted for custom suits to wear on-air for the television ministry, or dating the women who are flocking to him. It's not the kind of news you want to leave on voice mail."

So that was it. Deacon Ames couldn't get spiritual guidance from his spiritual leader. Obviously some of the Standing Rock members who had been frequenting New Hope couldn't either.

Micah didn't mind standing in at all. This man had once been a mentor and a great help to him when he first arrived at Standing Rock. The bad blood between them needed to flow away. Micah was going to pray away any lingering animosity today.

"Deacon, I'm sorry to hear about the cancer," he said. "You can call me anytime you need me. If I'm not available right away, someone here will track me down or pray with you in my place. Let's go to the throne of God."

The men knelt in front of their chairs and bowed their heads. When Micah had helped Deacon Ames rise and retrieve his cane, he offered the deacon the chair again.

Deacon Ames shook his head and walked toward the door.

"No, I've taken enough of your time. Thank you so much for the prayer, Reverend. You and I both know that the prayers of the righteous are powerful. You are clearly walking in God's favor."

Micah looked at Deacon Ames's sorrowful eyes and hesitated. He didn't know how serious the cancer was or whether he would see him again, so he went ahead and spoke the words God was urging him to share.

"Deacon, thank you for coming to me today. It meant a lot to see you again and to pray with you. I'll be checking on you, but I want you to leave here certain of this: What may have been meant for bad has turned out to be for better. All that Standing Rock stuff is old news; I am where the Lord wants me to be. No regrets, no grudges."

Deacon Ames turned back to hug Micah fiercely before opening the door and shuffling away on his cane.

Serena, Erika, Tawana, and Ms. Carter had been sitting in the hall with the children, waiting on Micah to emerge. They looked from Deacon Ames to Micah and back again.

"Did I just see who I thought I saw?" Serena asked as she rose from her seat and walked toward her husband.

Micah pulled his wife into his arms.

"Daddy is something else, Serena. That's all I can say."

44

As the women bustled in the kitchen that afternoon, working together to prepare dinner, Deacon Ames's visit remained the hot topic.

Each of them was stunned by his emotional exit.

"Things must be bad over at Standing Rock," Erika said as she chopped cabbage. "That's what they get for treating Micah the way they did."

Serena, who was making macaroni and cheese, frowned. "Let's not go there," she said. "You know how furious I was right after they fired Micah, but we've moved on. If the church is still there and spreading a message to people every Sunday, both in the building and over TV, I just pray that it's coming from God's Word. Otherwise a lot of people are going to get hurt."

"Like Deacon Ames," Ms. Carter interjected.

"That's what worries me more than anything," Serena said. "The people who have been faithful members of that congregation for years may be finding out that what they've put their faith and trust in isn't of God."

Ms. Carter was sitting at the kitchen table, stirring a bowl of ingredients to make cornbread. "When that happens, though, Serena, maybe they can find their way back to the one true God. All of us here know the truth shall set you free. You can't walk in darkness forever. God's light always shines through, so we don't have to worry about what's going on over there; God's going to take care of it."

Tawana looked at her mother. "When did you become an evangelist?"

Everyone, including Ms. Carter, laughed. She shrugged her shoulders.

"This summer in Richmond has been a good one," Ms. Carter said. "I've learned a lot attending church with Ms. Brenda and coming to New Hope occasionally. I've found myself reading the Good Book more. But I've also kept my ear to the streets. I know what's going on in the dark too."

Serena looked at Ms. Carter and raised an eyebrow. "Who you got dirt on?"

Ms. Carter smiled and shook her head. "It doesn't matter; we're all on a journey, and it takes some of us longer to get there than others. We have to be patient with each other and love each other no matter what."

Tawana, who had been stirring a pot of hot water filled with tea bags, laid her wooden spoon on a dishcloth and walked over to sit at the table across from her mother. Her eyes filled with tears. "You know, don't you?"

Ms. Carter looked at her daughter tenderly. "Do you know what your middle name means?"

Tears slid down Tawana's cheeks. She shook her head.

"*Elise* means 'God is my oath' by some definitions and 'Belonging to God' in others," Ms. Carter said. She chuckled.

"I didn't know that myself when I gave you that name, but that's another sign of the role God plays in our destiny. Serena had one of those baby name books lying around, and I picked it up one afternoon when I was babysitting.

"When I heard that you were going by 'T. Elise Carter' at work, I was really hurt that 'Tawana' wasn't good enough," she said. "It made me feel like I wasn't good enough for you anymore, and that once you got your law degree, you'd run from everything in your past, including me and Misha."

Tawana raised her eyes. "I'm sorry, Mama. I'd never do that."

Serena and Erika had joined the mother and daughter at the table.

"Never say never, baby," Ms. Carter said softly. "We hope that we won't do certain things, but when we find ourselves in tough situations, we never know what will surface. Did you plan well ahead of time to alter your name?"

Tawana bowed her head.

Ms. Carter reached across the table and covered Tawana's hand with hers.

"It really doesn't matter, Tawana," she said. "I've been told how tough it can be in the corporate world. You do what feels best. Elise is part of your name. Use it, if that's what you prefer."

She went back to stirring her cornbread. "Just so you know, though, 'Tawana' is perfect for you, too. It means 'tan hide' or 'created.'"

The women erupted in laughter.

"Let me find one of my books," Serena said between her giggles. "Let's all double check our names."

When they had settled down, Serena stood awkwardly, with her growing belly, and hugged Ms. Carter's neck.

"It's so good to have some wisdom at the table," Serena said. "I've been wanting to say something to T about all the calls we had been getting for 'Elise,' but I didn't know how without sounding like her mama."

Tawana sighed. "I don't know why I did that. I got to Wallace, Jones and Johns that first day and for some reason felt inadequate." She looked at her mother sheepishly. "I felt like my name told them more about me than my Harvard education could mask. I'm struggling with trying not to be ashamed of my past, both the things that happened here and things I've done at Harvard, but it all seems to be catching up to me."

"What do you mean, T?" Serena asked.

"I can't tell you much right now, because it has to do with Neal Lewis's murder case," Tawana said. She looked at her mother and took her hand.

"Some of it may become public, Mama, and it may be embarrassing, but I hope you can forgive me," she said. "You're right; I'm going to have to deal with my past and confront the truth head on. That's the only way the shadows are going to lose their power."

45

Erika waited until Gabrielle returned the phone to its cradle, and then walked over to her office.

"Got a minute?"

"Sure, what's up?"

Erika leaned against the door frame and looked at the clock on the wall. "Can you take an early lunch? I need to talk."

Gabrielle checked the calendar on her Blackberry.

"My next appointment isn't until two," she said. "I'm all yours."

They wound up at Sine' Irish Restaurant in Shockoe Slip, where they both ordered the fish and chips.

"You okay?" Gabrielle asked between sips of sweet tea. "I've noticed you poking around the office this week looking pitiful, and in the evenings too, when I've stayed at your house."

Erika laughed. "What kind of friend and colleague are you? You waited all week to ask."

Gabrielle gave her a knowing look. "I figure it has something to do with Derrick or Elliott; I wanted to give you your space until you were ready to talk."

"Has Derrick been in touch?"

"About the business, sure," Gabrielle said. "But he's called every day this week, when I usually hear from him once or twice, except through email. And each time, he asks, 'How's Erika?' and moves on to something else."

Erika leaned toward Gabrielle.

"What have you told him?" she asked with urgency.

Gabrielle smiled. "Don't worry, I haven't mentioned how you've been acting like a sick puppy. He knows you're busy with the Short Pump account; that's the story I've stuck to all week, without revealing anything personal."

Erika sagged in her seat. "Thanks."

"What is going on? Are you two finally trying to get together, now that you've made up your mind about Elliott? If so, what's with all the coyness? You're both grown. Call that man up and tell him you love him. He'll take the lead from there."

Erika looked miserably at Gabrielle. "I tried that already and it backfired. He's already taken. I waited until it was too late."

Gabrielle frowned.

"Taken? Derrick? Not after . . ." She caught herself. "Never mind. I promised both of you a long time ago that what you told me would stay with me unless you gave me permission to share."

Gabrielle looked pointedly at Erika. "I don't know what you've heard or have been told, but you need to double check your information."

Erika shook her head. The waitress placed a heaping

plate of food in front of her, and although it smelled delicious, she suddenly wasn't hungry.

"I need your help, Gabrielle. I have to find a job with another interior design firm. I'm going to have to quit this one."

46

Neal Lewis's day in court had finally arrived. It was as much a pivotal day for Tawana as it was going to be for him.

The bailiff declared the court in session. Everyone rose, including Neal, flanked by his team of lawyers, when Judge Roberts entered.

They were instructed to take their seats before the court clerk detailed Neal's charge of first-degree murder and the accompanying crime.

Bob Wallace, Kent Jones, and Vincent Johns stood with Neal when he answered the charge as he had during his arraignment several months earlier.

He said the words clearly and confidently: "Not guilty."

Murmuring filled the courtroom. Judge Roberts banged his gavel to silence them.

Knowing how Drew died, Tawana also cringed. She calmed herself by reflecting on what was to come. She and this team had spent hours hammering out their strategy, and finally, she had been able to sleep at night, confident that in staying on the case, she wasn't outside of God's will.

Tawana turned and surveyed the courtroom, which was packed with Drew's family and friends on her left, and Neal's family and friends on the right, just behind the defense team. TV, radio, and newspaper reporters were scattered between both groups.

Tawana gasped when she saw her mother and Serena sitting in a far corner of the gallery on the last row of seats. They smiled in encouragement.

Bethany and Ian were there, sitting opposite Serena and Ms. Carter. Victoria had been called as a witness and couldn't sit in the courtroom, but obviously her parents had come to support her.

Tawana surmised that Bethany, who was wearing oversized tinted shades that hid most of her face, was going to listen to all she could and coach her daughter before Victoria took the witness stand. She wondered if she should alert Bob, Kent, or Vincent and suggest that Bethany be restricted from the courtroom too.

Before she could decide, she saw him. He sat in the middle of the fifth row and stared at her. When their eyes met, he gave her a weak smile.

Seeing Grant Parker took her back to a night she wanted expunged from her history.

Tawana took a deep breath and remembered Mama's words from a few weeks earlier: *We hope that we won't do certain things, but when we find ourselves in tough situations, we never know what will surface.*

Tawana scribbled a note on her pad and passed it to Arlen, who sat next to her.

He's here.

Arlen read it, wrote a brief response, and returned his attention to Judge Roberts, who was giving the twelve jurors trial instructions.

Tawana swiftly read his one-word reply: *Perfect.*

47

On the third day of the trial, Prosecutor Scott Rodham called Victoria to the witness stand.

Rodham and his team had interrogated everyone from Neal's best friend, Steele, to several dozen teens who met Neal at Victoria's pool party. Some of them testified to witnessing the hostile exchange between Neal and Drew.

When she had been sworn in, Victoria recounted the story she had shared with authorities in recent weeks, after her connection to Neal had been leaked to the media.

"He was cute, he was nice, and I was glad he came to my party," she said. "I hadn't told my parents about him because they knew I sort of liked Drew, and Drew had been coming around. My dad would not have liked me dating two guys at the same time."

She hesitated and looked at Ian.

"Plus, he didn't know I had gone to Washington, D.C., and met Neal. I went with one of my girlfriends from school, on an afternoon that Daddy thought I had a modeling session. On the day of my party, Neal and Drew argued; but when I left them in the pool house utility room, they were talking sports," Victoria continued, as Scott Rodham led her through the sequence of events leading up to Drew's disappearance. "I came back about twenty minutes later and they were gone. I thought they had decided to leave together because they were angry with me for dating both of them.

"Neal didn't call me for a couple of days, but I had expected him to snub me and play hard to get," Victoria said and shrugged. "When I heard Drew was missing, I didn't connect the two guys. I mean, we're teenagers; who would get mad enough over a girl to kill someone?"

Tawana gave Victoria credit: she was innocent, beautiful, and convincing. When she left the witness stand, Ian and Bethany walked out of the courtroom with her, hugging her.

The prosecution informed the judge that Victoria was their final witness. They were resting their case on the strength of her testimony. After a lunch break, the Wallace, Jones, and Johns team would present its defense.

Ninety minutes later, Neal sat before the jury, trying to contain his nervousness. He continually brushed away a strand of hair that flopped over his forehead.

Tawana gave him a thumbs-up, then surveyed the courtroom. Victoria and Ian were nowhere in sight, but Bethany, still hiding behind her shades, had returned. Tawana passed a note to the bailiff in the rear of the courtroom.

Neal glued his eyes to Kent, who led the questioning, and told his version of how he and Victoria met, why he kept sneaking to Richmond to visit her, and why he had been upset on the day of the party to find Drew there, claiming to be her date.

Then Neal dropped the bombshell.

Bethany leaned forward in her seat while he spoke, as if she were straining to hear.

"I pinned Drew down with one of my wrestling moves and held him there," Neal told Kent. "I guess I blanked out. The next thing I knew, Victoria was standing over me, trying to pull me off of him. She asked me what I had done."

Neal looked toward Bethany, who had risen from her seat and was pointing at him with a French-manicured nail.

"You stop lying on my daughter!" she screamed.

Judge Roberts pounded his gavel and ordered the bailiff to remove her from the courtroom. Arlen stood and asked to be recognized.

"Your Honor, if we could keep a deputy with her to make sure she doesn't leave the premises, that would be helpful. As you'll hear shortly, she may be an integral part of this case."

Intrigued, Judge Roberts complied. "Call Deputy Woodson and tell him to wait with her in the interview room next door."

Kent asked Neal to continue.

"Drew wasn't moving. He just lay there, with his eyes open, but fixed." Neal's voice began to crack. "Victoria was about to run for help when her mother came in and saw Drew on the ground. Victoria told her she was going to call 911, but Mrs. Miller stopped her. She said she didn't want to ruin the party by calling an ambulance."

A low roar of gasps and murmuring filled the courtroom. Tawana sat back in her chair and folded her arms.

She had no doubt this boy was telling the truth; he had Bethany pegged.

"She said she didn't want to ruin the party?" Kent repeated.

Neal nodded. "She forced Victoria to go out and mingle with her friends and told Victoria that she and I would figure out what to do."

Neal shook his head at the memory. Tears filled his eyes, and he looked at jurors.

"Since I'm trained in CPR, I checked his pulse and tried to revive him," he said. "But Mrs. Miller stopped me. She said we couldn't have ambulances and police coming to her house. So . . ."

He bowed his head and lowered his voice.

"Speak up, son," Kent said gently.

"By the time I finished arguing with her about how crazy that was, there was no hope. I tried CPR for about five minutes and got no response."

Neal looked up again, but this time at his family and at Drew's. "I'm so sorry. I didn't mean to, but I killed Drew Thomas, and I helped Mrs. Miller hide his body."

48

Serena couldn't move. The judge had ordered a recess, and the families and other spectators filed into the courtroom lobby. However, she was glued to her seat.

Bethany Miller had aided in the commission of a murder? The wife of her husband's best friend? A socialite mother?

She pinched herself to make sure she wasn't dreaming, or suffering from "baby brain" pregnancy hallucinations.

Ms. Carter, who sat next to her, was speechless, too. "I'll never watch another episode of *Law and Order* in the same way," she said, trying to lighten the mood. Then, "What kind of profession has my daughter gotten herself into?"

Serena knew she couldn't use the cell phone inside the courtroom, so she forced herself to join the throng outside.

Reporters with notepads were jotting down comments from friends and relatives who had just heard Neal's testimony. Some were asking them to speak into mini-recorders. Others were on cell phones, filling in editors or producers on the recent development.

She tried to find a quiet spot to call Micah.

"Hey, babe," she said when she reached him, "you need to get here quick, for Ian. He's going to need you."

"You called me before I could call you," Micah responded. "I've already talked to Ian, and I'm on my way to the courthouse to meet him."

"He heard about Bethany already?"

There was a long pause before Micah responded. "I'm not sure what you're talking about, but they've asked him to bring Victoria back for further questioning. He's worried."

Serena sighed. "He should be. Get here as fast as you can."

49

Court resumed with Bob Wallace's request to call a surprise witness.

Scott Rodham objected to someone whose name wasn't revealed in the discovery phase of the trial being allowed to testify.

Bob convinced Judge Roberts that the witness, who had only recently surfaced, was significant.

Tawana held her breath when Grant Parker's name was called. He walked to the witness stand with his head lowered and his hands shoved in his pockets.

The series of questions and answers began with him identifying himself as a Harvard medical student, with an emphasis in plastic surgery. He explained that this was his first visit to Richmond, then acknowledged that he had relatives in the area with whom he had recently been in contact.

"With whom have you been talking and corresponding via email?"

"My aunt," was Grant's nervous reply.

"What is her name?"

"Bethany Miller."

"Did you two talk regularly before this summer?"

"Not really, except for holidays and birthdays," Grant said. "She called me sometime in June to say hello and invite me to visit the family, since I was spending my summer just a couple of hours away, in North Carolina."

Bethany had inquired about his studies at Harvard and asked if, by chance, he knew Tawana, whom she had recently met through a couple she knew.

"I asked her why, but Aunt Bethany never really answered," Grant said. "She went on and on about how nice Tawana was and mentioned that Tawana was working with a prominent Richmond law firm for the summer, on a big case. She hinted that I should come up and take Tawana out."

Grant looked briefly in Tawana's direction, before continuing.

"I mentioned that I had had a brief relationship with Tawana, and Aunt Bethany seemed thrilled.

"When I asked her why she was so interested in my love life all of a sudden, she stumbled over her words, but then she asked me again to come up to Richmond to see Tawana.

"Aunt Bethany can usually steamroll her plans through, but I couldn't let that happen this time," Grant said. "I told her that Tawana and I hadn't parted as friends. She kept pressuring me for details, and I don't know why, but I told her some things that I hadn't shared with anyone else. She seemed elated after I had spilled my guts, and instead of making me feel better about some bad choices, she rushed me off the phone. Later that week, I picked up a copy of the *The Washington Post* and read that a Harvard law student, T. Elise Carter, was helping with a big murder trial in Richmond. I knew it had to be Tawana. And I remembered some shameful things I'd said to Tawana about her name."

Tawana turned to look at her mother and Serena. With her eyes, she pleaded with them to leave. Ms. Carter shook her head and mouthed, "It's okay" to her daughter.

Tawana closed her eyes and waited for Grant's full revelation. She was startled when someone reached for her hand and squeezed it.

She opened her eyes and looked into Arlen's reassuring ones.

Bob cleared his throat. "What was this great news Mrs. Miller had received during your chat?"

"I confided in Aunt Bethany that I had taken Tawana on a date and that at the end of night . . ." He paused and looked apologetically at Tawana, who with Arlen's support, had decided to face the music with her eyes open.

She returned Grant's gaze but showed no emotion.

"Go on, sir," Bob prodded.

"I had asked Tawana if she wanted to go back to my apartment and she indicated that she would—for a price."

Judge Roberts was forced to bang the gavel again, to restore order in the courtroom.

Tawana looked at Serena and her mother again. Ms. Carter's eyes were closed. Serena nodded at Tawana and slightly smiled. At least they hadn't fled in shame.

"Did you sleep with Tawana Elise Carter during your date?"

Grant answered softly. "Yes, I did."

"Did you pay Tawana Elise Carter for sex that night?"

Grant looked at Tawana and spoke firmly. "No, I did not. It was strictly consensual."

"Is Tawana Elise Carter a prostitute?"

"No, sir," Grant answered. "Not to my knowledge. I, too, bear some of the blame for what happened that night."

50

Bob Wallace quickly had Grant ushered out of the courtroom and put Neal back in the witness seat.

"You are still under oath," Bob told him.

Neal nodded to indicate that he understood.

"We heard your earlier testimony about how you didn't mean to seriously injure Drew Thomas and how Mrs. Miller coerced you into going along with her plan," Bob said. "Why didn't you go to the police instead?"

"When Mrs. Miller showed up in the utility room to break up the argument between Drew and me, I told her that my dad was Walker Lewis. I could tell right away that she knew he was a Washington bigwig," Neal said.

"I knew that was why she said I could stay at the party but Drew had to leave.

"She supervised me as I rolled Drew's body in some pool tarp and lifted it onto a delivery cart in the utility room. As she watched for guests, I rolled the cart to her SUV and put Drew in the back. Mrs. Miller drove along some back roads to a secluded spot, and along the way told me that she and her husband had interacted with my parents several times during social events hosted by the D.C. Chapter of Stanford alumni.

"Mrs. Miller had graduated from the university as well, but since there wasn't a chapter in Richmond, she and her husband would participate in the D.C. functions, for networking purposes." Neal recounted the information as if he were delivering a school report.

Bob interrupted. "So you were intimidated by this woman because she might run into your parents at an alumni event and 'tell' on you?"

Neal shook his head.

"She knew that my dad was under consideration by the President to join the Federal Reserve System's Board of Governors. After a presidential appointment, Dad would still have to be confirmed by the Senate, which would mean the entire family would be under scrutiny.

"If the media or political officials inside the Washington Beltway got wind of what I had done, my dad's career could be over," Neal said. "Mrs. Miller promised to make that happen if I didn't do as she said."

Neal looked into the courtroom gallery at his father, who sat just behind the defense table with his lips pursed and his arms folded, glaring at his son.

"Go on," Bob prodded.

Neal was visibly shaken by his father's demeanor, but returned his focus to his attorney.

"Mrs. Miller had talked to my mom at one of the alumni functions and knew that I had been accepted to Stanford. She said her brother was a Stanford grad and San Franscisco-based plastic surgeon who sat on the university's admissions board. She didn't come right out and threaten me, but I took what she did say to mean that he could get my admission to the college revoked," Neal said. "That would kill my parents."

"She knew so much about my family that I believed her threats," he said. "She had my dad's dream job and my future in her hands. She promised me that if I kept quiet and went along with her plan, we'd never get caught."

"But you did," Bob said.

Earlier testimony from Richmond detectives revealed that a silver pendant bearing the Seward School emblem had been found in Drew's shallow grave. Strands of auburn hair were lifted from his clothing.

Neal continued with his testimony, stating that Bethany Miller still didn't relent.

"She visited me in jail and promised that if I insisted I was innocent, there would be enough reasonable doubt to get me off," Neal said. "She came back a few weeks later and told me she had some dirt on one of my attorneys that we could use to secure my freedom or to get the charge against me lessened.

"Mrs. Miller said that Elise's real name was Tawana and that she had come close to breaking the law herself. She was counting on the fact that Elise would help us out to save her own skin." Neal shook his head. "At that point, I just didn't trust her anymore.

"My mom came to visit me and told me she would stand by me no matter what happened. I decided to come clean."

Neal looked at his father. "I'm sorry it cost me the love of my dad. But at least now I can sleep at night."

51

Victoria returned to the witness stand and admitted to being present when Drew died.

The girl wept uncontrollably as she described how her mother had prevented her from calling 911.

"She told me to suck it up, to smile, and to go back to the party," Victoria sobbed. "She told me to keep the other kids distracted so they wouldn't see her and Neal leaving with Drew's body."

"How were you able to pull that off, knowing Drew was lying there dead, just feet away, inside that utility room?" Vincent Johns asked.

"I think I was in shock," Victoria said. "I couldn't believe my mother was doing something like this.

"She was afraid for my father to find out that she was throwing me a party. He had told her to cut back on spending, but he was out of town on business that weekend. She spent thousands that night alone, all because I had begged for this party," Victoria said, as the tears flowed. "I felt guilty; if I hadn't wanted a big bash, I wouldn't have put my mother, Neal, or Drew in this position."

Vincent continued his questioning. "Why was your financially successful father, a leader in the banking industry, concerned about money, given his lucrative career and the exclusive area in which you lived?"

"Mom confided in me that she had overextended herself on credit and that Daddy had no idea how serious it was," Victoria said.

Ian, who had been in the courtroom since Grant testified, sat shell-shocked. Tawana wasn't sure if he was still listening.

"She loved to shop and could spend up to three or four thousand dollars a week, if not every few days," Victoria said matter-of-factly. "We liked to look good and have a good time."

When jurors filed out of the courtroom so Judge Roberts could speak privately with the attorneys, Bob requested that, given the circumstances, Neal be offered a plea agreement.

"Your star witness just sat up there and perjured herself," Bob told Scott Rodham.

The city's top prosecutor couldn't argue.

At nine o'clock the next morning, Neal Lewis pleaded guilty to the lesser crime of manslaughter, based on the fact that Drew Thomas's killing was committed in the heat of passion and not premeditated, and that Neal had tried to revive his victim. Neal would be sentenced in six weeks and face one to ten years in prison instead of twenty to life.

Drew Thomas's parents had been informed of the agreement before court went into session. After the terms of the plea were read aloud, Neal asked to address them. He looked at Drew's weeping mother and began to bawl.

Across the aisle, his own mother shed tears. Neal's father refused to make eye contact with him.

"I am so sorry for all the lives I have ruined," Neal said. "If I could go back in time and just walk away, I would. I would. I am so sorry. If you can find it your hearts, please forgive me."

Drew's extended family and friends filed silently from the courtroom, holding on to each other. His parents were the last to leave. When Drew's mother reached the door, which the bailiff held open for her, she turned and looked at Neal, who had returned to his seat at the defense table and sat there with his head bowed.

Mrs. Thomas called out to him.

"Neal?" She dabbed her eyes with her tissue and waited for him to look her way.

Slowly, he did.

Judge Roberts watched but didn't interrupt. The courtroom was silent.

"My son was a good kid," she said softly. "The best part about him was that he loved God. He would want me to pray for you, so I will."

With that, she was gone.

○

Neal shook hands and traded hugs with his slew of attorneys before being led back to jail.

"Thank you all for what you did for me. I could have been facing life."

Tawana embraced him tightly. "Remember what I told you—it's who you are inside that counts," she said. "Don't let prison turn you into someone you don't want to be."

Neal didn't respond.

Anything he said right now wouldn't matter much anyway, she realized. He was at the oyster stage; how he handled the rest of his long journey would determine what he became.

The same would be true for Victoria, who had been taken into custody and sent to the city's juvenile detention center for girls. She would be arraigned in two days on accessory to murder charges.

"I'm sorry, Daddy," she said through her tears as she was led away.

Bethany went kicking and screaming. "This is a mistake! Neal is a liar. Grant is a liar, and someone has brainwashed my daughter! I can't go to jail! I'll die! Please, somebody help me!"

Ian had sat in the courtroom until the courthouse was nearly empty. When he failed to emerge after half an hour, Tawana went to retrieve him.

She sat in the seat next to him and bowed her head, as his was.

"I'm really sorry," she said softly.

"I know," he said. "I've lost my entire family. And for what? A glamorous image? A hip pool party? My wife's secret spending habits? Why is God doing this to me?"

Tawana didn't have ready answers.

"You aren't the one going to jail, Ian," she finally said. "Unfortunately, you have to suffer because of someone else's choices. As you heard during the trial, I made wrong ones too, but I have to believe that God is bigger than any problems either of us is going to face because of what happened in court today."

Ian kept his head bowed. "Maybe, maybe not. Can I be alone?"

Tawana left the courtroom and asked the deputy to give Ian ten more minutes. The sobs she heard as the door swung closed behind her told her he needed every second.

52

"orry I'm late, but you have to read this," Erika waved a greeting card in Serena's face. "Where is Tawana? I need some legal advice."

"Calm down," Serena said. "What is it?"

Serena took the card from Erika and rested her hands on her stomach, which was growing larger by the day.

Serena's head snapped up. "Elliott has lost his mind."

Erika nodded. "Now you see why I'm late. The potato salad and lemon pound cake were ready to go. But when I opened this card and read the documents folded inside, I lost it."

Serena shook her head. "I wouldn't be too worried. Elliott will be in jail for at least three more months for assaulting Mara. This request for visitation won't wind its way through the court system by then," she said. "I'm not a lawyer, but I'm sure of that."

Tawana entered the kitchen with an empty plate in her hand.

"The ribs are smokin', Serena," she said. "Micah put his foot in them! Why are you two in here looking so pensive?"

"Elliott is suing me for visitation rights," Erika said. "He's trying to force me to bring Aaron to see him while he's incarcerated."

"Elliott has lost his mind," Tawana said.

Serena laughed. "You've been living here too long; you're starting to sound like me."

"Ah, so that's why you're throwing me a farewell party," Tawana teased.

The late August barbecue was serving numerous purposes.

It was indeed a farewell gathering for Tawana, Misha, and Ms. Carter, who would be returning to Boston soon; but it was also a welcome-to-Richmond party for Micah's sister Evelyn, who had arrived that morning for a two-week visit with her children, Zuri and Tyra. Although their scheduled summer visit had been delayed by an emergency at the day-care center Evelyn operated, she had been determined to come.

The barbecue was also a thank-you celebration for New Hope's ministry leaders, who had been so wonderful during the transition from Stillwell Elementary to Zion Memorial. The backyard was overflowing with food, music, and mingling men, women, and children. Serena's dad was there with Althea and Kami. Rev. Tolliver, the pastor of Zion Memorial, had come with his wife, Ruth.

Tawana looked out of the kitchen window and burst into laughter. A youth leader from New Hope was trying to teach the Tollivers the electric slide.

"I think Reverend Tolliver's got it! He doesn't wear a pacemaker does he?"

Serena swatted Tawana's head and peeked over her shoulder at the dancing minister. "Behave yourself, girl. Here come your friends from the law firm."

Tawana turned to Erika. "Don't worry, Erika. With Elliott's abuse history and the fact that he's behind bars, there's very little chance that he can force you to take Aaron to the city jail for visits. Before he is released, I'd advise you to request from the court that he be required to complete individual counseling and parenting classes before he can see Aaron again. For the time being, though, you're okay."

Erika sighed and mouthed "Thank you."

Tawana smiled and headed for the door. "No problem; let me go say hello to Arlen."

"Just Arlen?" Serena asked, one eyebrow arched.

Tawana paused and smiled. "Let me greet *all* of my friends, including my bosses."

She stepped outside and Serena turned to Erika. "Feel better?"

Erika nodded and hugged her. "It's been a rough few weeks, with the drama from Elliott and, well, you know."

Erika picked up the Pyrex dish of potato salad she had made. "I'll take this outside."

"Not so fast," Serena said. "Someone on the patio wants to talk to you."

Serena slid the door open and stuck her head outside.

"She's here," she said.

Erika almost dropped the food when Derrick—and the striking woman who had been at his home last month—entered the kitchen.

Serena swooped the dish from Erika's arms and disappeared.

The woman stepped forward and extended her hand.

"Erika, I'm Delaney. Derrick's cousin."

53

Y ou fled from the house before I could introduce you,"
Derrick said, and stood at his cousin's side. "Delaney
recently moved here from Michigan to enroll in grad school
at Catholic University. She stopped by to visit me for a few
days last month and scout out an apartment for the fall
semester."

Erika felt like a bug. She wanted to squash herself. How
had Serena convinced them to come?

Delaney smiled gingerly. "I came prancing into the foyer
that morning like I was the lady of the house, on purpose,"
she said. "I've seen all these women throwing themselves
at my first cousin. He's good looking, successful, and single.
He needs me around to help him weed through the women
who just want a sugar daddy."

Derrick rolled his eyes, but let her continue.

"That morning when you showed up, in your sundress
and sandals looking like a miniature Barbie, I wanted to
size you up before he fell for whatever lines you might
use to reel him in."

Erika wasn't sure if she liked Delaney, but she appreciated that this cousin was so protective of Derrick.

"Technically, Delaney," she said, "that *is* why I was there."

Delaney nodded. "If I had known it was you, I would have handed you the fishing rod," she said softly. "The only time I've seen Derrick's eyes light up is when he talks about a woman, who just happens to be an employee, named Erika. When Gabrielle told him two weeks ago that you were planning to leave the design firm and that he might not have an excuse to see you again, he was sick.

"I wanted to call you, but Derrick said you weren't responding to his messages," Delaney said, "and hearing from me might make things worse."

Derrick kept his eyes on Erika but touched Delaney's shoulder.

"Thanks, cuz; you've said enough," he said. "Maybe too much."

Delaney looked from him to Erika and headed for the patio.

"Nice to meet you, Erika," she said before stepping outside. "I hope I'll see you again."

When she was gone, Derrick turned to Erika. "She's a little over the top, but she can't help it. She's majoring in theater and dance."

Erika wanted to laugh, but the other emotions tumbling inside of her prevented her from expressing herself.

She was angry, confused, hopeful.

"I know," Derrick said. He had read it all in her eyes. He pulled her trembling body toward him and hugged her.

"I'm sorry," she whispered as she rested her head against

his chest. "I'm sorry that it took me so long to say this, but I love you."

Derrick closed his eyes and rested his chin on the top of her head. "So, you aren't going to quit your job?"

Erika smiled.

"Make me a counteroffer."

54

Tawana strolled across the lawn toward her colleagues. She could have picked up her pace, but she was purposely savoring this moment.

Bob, Kent, and Vincent didn't care whether she went by Tawana or Elise. They learned just before Neal's trial about her connection to Grant and the secret Bethany was trying to use to blackmail her. They knew she was a single mother.

Still, they each told her, she was one of them.

"You're an excellent attorney, and I hope you aren't looking to go somewhere else next summer," Bob had said two nights ago during a dinner the firm hosted for the summer clerks. "Richmond is your home, and so is our firm—if you'd like it to be."

And then there was Arlen. He had shown Tawana what it meant to have a man as a friend. He challenged her intellectually and pushed her to question the depth of her faith.

"Don't just believe something about God because you

heard it in a sermon or because someone you admire told you," he had said one afternoon over lunch. "Ask the hard questions. Read the Bible for yourself and try to figure out what was going on in the culture when those particular passages were written. Know God for yourself."

He shared his long-term goals with Tawana and even his doubts. He let her help him plan a solo trip to South Africa and Ghana, where he would be going in two weeks to celebrate his thirtieth birthday.

Most important, Arlen gave her the freedom to be herself.

"I don't care what you call yourself—Tawana, T. Elise, or 'Tay Tay,'" he had joked. "You shouldn't get hung up on that. Tawana and T. Elise can be the same powerful, beautiful person, with no apologies. You do what feels right."

Life at Harvard was going to be so much easier after this summer. She just knew it.

Tawana introduced the law partners and the other summer clerks to Micah and Serena and led them to the table laden with food and beverages. Then she excused herself.

"I need to take care of something," she told Bob. "I'll be back shortly."

Tawana found Misha choreographing cheer routines for some of the girls from New Hope, who had come to the party with their parents. She tapped her daughter on the shoulder and whispered in her ear. "Can someone take over for you just for a few minutes? I need to talk with you."

Misha smiled. Whenever her mother wanted her attention, she was willing to give it.

She took Tawana's hand and strolled with her to their

bedroom. Misha sat at the end of the bed and rested her sneakered feet on the stepladder that she used each night to climb onto the elevated mattress and springboard.

"What's up, Mommy?"

Tawana sat next to Misha and kissed her cheek. "Sorry to interrupt you during the party, but I couldn't wait any longer to share this with you."

Misha looked at her expectantly.

"You've been so patient with me these past few years, Misha, and I know it's been hard," Tawana said. "Even this summer, this murder trial consumed a lot of my time."

Misha hugged Tawana. "That's okay, Mommy. I had so much fun with Aunt Serena and with the twins. They're like my little brothers now."

Tawana smiled and ran her palm across her daughter's braided hair, smoothing it into place.

"We're heading back to Boston soon, and once again I'll be tied up with my classes and studying," she said. "But I don't want you to ever feel like you're not important to me again."

She sighed before continuing. "It's not going to be easy, Misha. Mommy has some hard work ahead of her, but I'm going to try to make time for us, even if it's just for a day, so that you and I can do something special together. Starting tomorrow."

Misha sat up. "What are we going to do?"

Tawana waved tickets in her hand. "Six Flags tomorrow; Ocean City, Maryland, the rest of the week—just you and me."

Misha squealed and hugged Tawana so tightly that Tawana couldn't breathe.

She pulled away and laughed. "I'm glad you're excited, baby. It's long overdue."

Misha was beaming. "Mommy, I love you. You're showing me who to be when I grow up. I'm going to make you proud."

They walked hand in hand to the backyard. Misha heard the beginning of the rap song "Chicken Noodle Soup" and took off toward her friends, who were creating a dance routine to the beat.

Tawana watched her and laughed, thankful that her daughter's childhood was already so different from her own. She looked in the other direction and saw her mother, who sat in a lawn chair, chatting and laughing with a member of the New Hope congregation.

Mama did her best then, and she's still giving me her all now. Thank you, God.

Out of the corner of her eye, she saw someone slowly open the fence and step into the backyard. He stood there until Micah, at the grill nearby, noticed him.

Micah passed his tongs to his father-in-law and walked over to Ian, whose eyes were red.

The men hugged for what seemed an eternity. Micah led Ian into the house. Tawana and Serena glanced at each other, and Serena nodded. Tawana knew what that meant.

Later tonight they would gather in prayer. For Ian.

55

Serena was satisfied.

This was one of those days she was thankful that God knew her heart, because she didn't know exactly what to pray.

She looked across the lawn at her boys, who were running and kicking a soccer ball with glee. Nothing else mattered in their world right now, except this moment in time.

How and when did adults stop being so in tune? Specifically, how and when had she?

She turned her gaze toward the sky, which was a clear azure blue, peppered with a cloud here and there. When had she stopped fully trusting God to paint the scenes of her life just as perfectly?

She rounded up Jaden and Jacob and hustled them inside for a potty break. Usually she fought with them to lie down and take their nap. It took at least thirty minutes to get them settled and another thirty before they were snoozing.

Today, though, she heard God clearly.

Rest.

After a light snack, she surprised the boys by taking them into her bedroom and lying between them.

"Naptime, guys; close your eyes."

Without a whimper both of them did. They snuggled close to her and, within minutes, both were sleeping soundly.

Serena thought about the dishes waiting for her in the sink; the bills on her desk that needed to be paid; the carpet she had planned to shampoo today.

This brief reprieve was when she usually played catch-up on the chores. But the stark revelations of the past month lingered with her. So did the blessings from the picnic she and Micah had hosted two weeks ago.

She hadn't flirted with selling her body like Tawana, or lost her life to preserve a fancy façade like Bethany. Yet just the same, she had been in danger of losing part of herself to something more sinister—to doubt and envy and the desire to be somewhere other than where she was right now.

She knew she didn't want to look back at these crazy, but tender, years with her family and find them a blur. She didn't want that to be the case with her relationship with God, either.

On this Monday midmorning, she thought about what she did want, like this baby squirming in her belly, her husband's deep kisses, and the scent of love that seemed to be ebbing and flowing in the lives of her friends and family. She wondered what kinds of pearls each of them was in the process of becoming.

Only God really knew, and for her, that was enough.

Watercolored Pearls
Discussion Questions

What does the book's title, *Watercolored Pearls*, convey about the characters?

What issues did the characters struggle with that, if openly addressed, could have strengthened their character? Deepened their relationships with each other? Drawn them closer to God?

What themes resonated throughout this book?

Was Serena's dislike of Bethany valid, or did it reveal her weaknesses and insecurity? As a pastor's wife, was it wrong for her to feel this way?

Was Serena's guilt about being overwhelmed with motherhood understandable? Did she have a superwoman (i.e., Proverbs 31 woman) complex?

Why was it hard for Tawana to open up to Serena, someone she had always believed loved her unconditionally?

Pearls aren't always formed naturally. Cultured pearls have outside help in being formed. How did the characters in this book help each other grow and mature?

Can you recall a personal situation or circumstance that transformed your character and/or your faith?

What role does faith play in helping one become a pearl?

Did any of these characters use their faith as a crutch, to keep them from growing and developing as they could have?

How has this book compelled you to reflect on the "pearls in progress" in your life and how you can nurture them?

Has this book encouraged you to view the parasites or "foreign objects" that are shaping you as blessings in disguise? If so, are you growing in a direction that pleases God?

Acknowledgments

This book is dear to my heart, not only because I loved writing about characters who were growing and maturing in faith and in the changing seasons of their lives, but also because it was a community labor of love.

Yes, I alone spent hours conducting research and sitting at my laptop writing, but without the tangible support and prayers of relatives, friends, colleagues, and readers, this project may not have left the idea stage. There are so many of you that I may neglect to mention you all. If so, please "charge it to my head, not to my heart!" For those I've mentioned in previous books, your support is still sincerely appreciated.

First and foremost, I thank God, my heavenly Father, for giving me the gift of writing and for birthing this book through me. I am grateful for the opportunity to pen stories that can encourage and transform readers.

As always, I thank my immediate and extended family, including my sisters and my in-laws, who are among my biggest cheerleaders. In particular, I thank my thoughtful husband, Donald, and my beloved children, for loving me and understanding when I must "steal away" to write or promote my work. Thank you for believing in me and in my ministry.

I sincerely thank Muriel Miller Branch for her prayers and for providing a sanctuary for me to write and meet my deadline. Many, many thanks to my fellow writer and author and my first reader, Sharon Shahid, who provided invaluable feedback and encouragement along the way. Special thanks is also due to my second reader, Carol Jackson, and to my Revell Books editor, Barb Barnes, for your thoughtful suggestions and insight.

I am also grateful to the following individuals: Jackie Ross Brown, Katrina Campbell, Pam Perry, Barbara L. Rascoe, Steve Laube, Gwendolyn Richard, Lori Willis, Patricia Haley, Sharon Ewell Foster, Kendra Norman-Bellamy, Marilyn Griffith, Fritz Kling, Linda Pate, Carol Mackey with Black Expressions Book Club, Gilda Squire, Sybil Wilkes with the *Tom Joyner Morning Show*, L. Marie Trotter, Stephanie Thomas, Robin Caldwell, members of Jack & Jill of Midlothian, Shaun Robinson, Dianne Burnett with Christianbook.com, Tyora Moody, Rod and Trevis Adams, J. T. and Catrina Murphy, Bobbie Walker Trussell, Claudia Mair Burney, Kathi Macias, Sharon Baldacci, Cecil Murphey, Helena Nyman, Gwen Mansini, Elli Sparks, Sally Ribeiro, Susan Davenport, Rachel Valenti, Kia Lee, Kimberly Dunham-Quigley, Tina Fox, Jeanette D. Phelps, Sabrina Harris, Althea Brooks, Ernestine Jolivet, and the Revell Books family, with special thanks to Brian Peterson, Lonnie Hull DuPont, Cat Hoort, Twila Bennett, Karen Steele, Deonne Beron, Nathan Henrion, Debbie Deacon, and the amazing cover art staff and sales team.

To the many bookstores, book clubs, individual readers, media professionals, and fellow writers who have supported my previous work and continue to spread the word about my writing, I sincerely appreciate you.

May each of you continue to grow in faith and character, in your quest to become the pearl God has destined you to be.

For His Glory,
Stacy